A Slender Thread

By the same author

MARCHWOOD
THE GOLDEN CAGE
APRIL WOOING
LAURIAN VALE
THE HOUSE OF CONFLICT
GAY INTRUDER
DIANA COMES HOME
A NEW LIFE FOR JOANNA
FAMILY GROUP
THE CONWAY TOUCH
THE FLOWERING YEAR
THE SECOND MRS RIVERS
FAIR PRISONER
ALEX AND THE RAYNHAMS
ROSEVEAN
COME LOVE, COME HOPE
THE FAMILY WEB
THE YOUNG ROMANTIC
A HOUSE WITHOUT LOVE
A DISTANT SONG
THE CHALLENGE OF SPRING
THE LYDIAN INHERITANCE
THE STEPDAUGHTER
THE QUIET HILLS
AN APRIL GIRL
ONLY OUR LOVE
THE MASTER OF HERONSBRIDGE
THE TANGLED WOOD
A SHELTERING TREE
ENCOUNTER AT ALPENROSE
A MAGIC PLACE
GOLDEN SUMMER
ROUGH WEATHER
THE BROKEN BOUGH
THE NIGHT OF THE PARTY
THE BEND IN THE RIVER
A HAUNTED LANDSCAPE
THE HAPPY FORTRESS
THE PATHS OF SUMMER
OLD LOVE'S DOMAIN
ONE DAY, MY LOVE

IRIS BROMIGE

A SLENDER THREAD

HODDER AND STOUGHTON
LONDON SYDNEY AUCKLAND TORONTO

British Library Cataloguing in Publication Data

Bromige, Iris
  A slender thread.
  I. Title
  823'.914[F]   PR6052.R572

ISBN 0-340-36628-1

Copyright © 1985 by Irish Bromige. First printed 1985. All rights reserved. No part of this publication may be reproduced or transmitted in any form or by any means, electronic or mechanical, including photocopy, recording, or any information storage and retrieval system, without permission in writing from the publisher. Printed in Great Britain for Hodder and Stoughton Limited, Mill Road, Dunton Green, Sevenoaks, Kent by The Thetford Press, Thetford, Norfolk. Typeset in Baskerville by Fleet Graphics, Enfield, Middlesex

Hodder and Stoughton Editorial Office: 47 Bedford Square, London WC1B 3DP

Contents

1	An Invitation	7
2	Christmas Eve	17
3	The Old Magic	23
4	Family Circle	35
5	A Business Proposition	41
6	Airborne	49
7	The Night of the Party	60
8	Mishaps	69
9	End of a Dream	84
10	Adrift	91
11	Revelations	98
12	Holiday Plans and Problems	108
13	Squalls	117
14	Misadventure	129
15	Getting It Straight	136
16	End of a Waiting Game	144

1
An Invitation

Rain was falling steadily from a grey November sky on to a road deserted except for a milk float. From the window of her flat, Kate Shetland surveyed this scene in a mood of depression mingled with exasperation. Another wet Saturday. Waiting for her breakfast coffee to percolate, she saw the postman, shrouded in plastic, wrestling with the ill-fitting gate, sending showers of spray from the overhanging privet hedge before hurrying up the path with several letters in his hand.

Probably nothing for her, she thought, as she rescued the toast, for there were three other flats besides hers in that Victorian house, and little correspondence came her way. But when she went out into the communal hall and riffled through the envelopes, there was one for her, and her heart lifted at the sight of Valerie's handwriting.

Sipping her coffee, she read,

Dear Kate,
    We are having a family party this Christmas and do so want you to join us, for we still look on you as one of the family, you know, in spite of your desertion these past two years. We have all missed you very much. Telephone chats are only a poor consolation. So please *do come*.
    If you feel that breaking off your engagement to Mark has caused a rift, think no more of it. Of course, it would have been nice to have you officially tied up with us, but none of us thinks of blaming you for changing your mind.

After all, Mark is not everyone's beau ideal for a husband – too bossy and can be extremely irritating – but that's no reason why you can't be friends and we can all be easy together as before. I know Mark will welcome you as we all will.

Mark, by the way, is bringing a (glamorous?) widow here for Christmas, with her four-year-old daughter. Her husband was Mark's chief at the Horticultural Station, and was tragically killed in a road accident six weeks ago. She is absolutely shattered, it seems, and Mark has persuaded her to spend Christmas with us, because Mother is so good with that sort of situation. And Mark has become Director of the Station, saddled suddenly with all sorts of new responsibilities, but I expect he'll cope with his usual competence. The little girl will be company for Evelyn's off-spring. So we shall have a house full, which, as you know, is how Mother likes it. but we do *especially* want you to come on Christmas Eve for as long as your job allows you. Please don't disappoint us. It will be like old times.

Love,
Valerie

P.S.   Quite forgot – the Touraine cousins will be coming on Christmas Day, too. Remember our holidays at the farm in Normandy? And how you and Philippe were inseparable? So you see you must come for a grand family reunion.

Kate smiled, hearing Valerie's quick, impetuous voice in the written words. Dear Valerie, who seemed to see life with such clear-eyed simplicity, when it was all so much more complex than that. But her postscript sent Kate's thoughts back to those holidays in France, looked forward to so fervently, relived during many a dark day in her own home. Her school friendship with Valerie Vermont had led to her being taken into the Vermont home and welcomed there with a warmth and affection that had ripened with the years. That Mrs. Vermont had known more of her home circum-

An Invitation

stances than she had at the time realised, and sought with characteristic kindness to compensate for them, had become clear to Kate as she grew up, although no word of criticism of her parents was ever passed. But she had become one of the Vermont family, and she owed them more than she could ever repay. They had brought happiness and laughter into her life, factors completely lacking in her own home.

Mrs. Vermont's sister Hester had married a French fruit farmer, Henri Touraine, and every summer the Vermonts had spent a fortnight at the old Normandy farmhouse, taking Kate with them for the first time when she was ten years old, and subsequently until she was seventeen, after which the Touraine children, Philippe and Madeleine, had spread their wings and left home, as had Mark and Evelyn on the English side, and the custom ceased. Individual visits were exchanged, but the old family holidays were outgrown. For Kate, though, Philippe lived on vividly in her memory. Dark complexioned, with unruly black hair, dark eyes and a flashing smile, he had looked to her like a gypsy when she had first met him. Thin and wiry, he had been full of energy, with a lively imagination that had made an immediate appeal to her, and they had become close companions. At sixteen she had fallen in love with him with all the romantic fervour of first love, too shy and uncertain to make her feelings known, hugging her secret to her and dreaming of him in the long gaps between holidays. He had remained friendly and affectionate, but made no effort to contact her during the gaps, and her one tentative letter had only received a scrawled postcard of few words in reply. She had fed hungrily on any words dropped about their cousin by the Vermonts, from which she learned that he had refused to become a farmer and carry on in his father's footsteps and had turned to the acting profession for a career, with some success. And so she had been left with her adolescent dreams which had never quite faded in the eight years that had elapsed since she had last seen him in spite of her engagement to Mark Vermont when she was twenty-one.

Her thoughts were still on Philippe later that morning

A Slender Thread

when a ring at her doorbell heralded her elder sister. Pamela came in on a waft of expensive perfume, immaculate as usual in a cherry red, well-tailored coat with black patent handbag and shoes, every black hair of her head lacquered into place in a smooth helmet round her pale-skinned face. She held out her red umbrella to Kate.

"Why doesn't somebody do something about that gate? I had a job to open it and got quite wet getting from the car to the entrance."

"Would you like some coffee?"

"No, thanks. I can't stop long. I've some shopping to do at Harrods. I just wanted to tell you about an opportunity for a good job that's cropped up and might suit you."

Pamela was eyeing her doubtfully, and Kate was aware of that old familiar experience of the role of a tiresome and unsatisfactory pupil up before a critical headmistress. She was conscious that her tweed skirt had long since lost any pretensions to stylishness, that her sweater had shrunk and that her thick hair was all over the place and needed trimming.

"Oh yes," she said warily.

"The Managing Director of a firm John has interests in is wanting a secretary, more of a personal assistant. John passed it on to me. You've got the intelligence and the qualifications for the job, but I just wonder whether you've got the drive and the personality. This man is a high-flyer, and it would be an exciting job. Lots of travel. Could lead anywhere. There's not much scope where you are. A pity you didn't take that other opening I found for you."

"Oh, my work for the charity organisation suits me as well as any office job in London would. I guess I'm not a high-flyer," concluded Kate with a wry little smile.

"That's a very negative attitude," said Pamela crisply. "You have to think of the future. John has quite a lot of influence and could get this job for you. You'd need to smarten yourself up a bit."

"I dressed this morning intending to get a train to Dorking and go walking in the Surrey hills," replied Kate, a little annoyed with herself for offering an explanation for her sartorial failings. "If the rain lets up, I may still go. I feel caged in here."

Pamela shrugged as though such plans were inexplicable, and took out a folded sheet of paper.

"I've typed out all the details of the job for you. Apply first in writing. If you can do it this weekend and bring it round to my flat on Monday evening, I'll vet it for you. It ought to go off early next week."

"I'll think about it," said Kate, and hastily went on as she saw her sister frown at this non-committal reception of her proposition, "I had a letter from Valerie this morning, asking me to spend Christmas with them. They're having a family party."

"You don't want to get mixed up with the Vermonts again, do you?"

"It's not a case of getting mixed up. They're my dearest friends, all of them."

"Well, really Kate, I did think that after you'd extricated yourself from that foolish engagement to Mark, your childish dependence on the Vermont family would be over. I never shared your enthusiasm for them."

"Without the Vermont family, I could never have endured our home life."

"That was grim, I know. You should have left home as I did."

"How could I leave Mother?"

"Well, that's all in the past. Now you're free and independent and don't need any escape."

"So I should ditch the friends who helped me through it?"

"You have, haven't you?" observed Pamela sweetly. "You've not seen them since you left Cheryton, have you?"

"I've kept in touch with Valerie. I haven't been to see them because somehow I've felt guilty at breaking with Mark. They would have been so disappointed. I hated to hurt them."

"What an odd way of looking at it! Surely you'd the right to refuse to marry a man, whatever family he belonged to. Sometimes I really cannot understand how your mind works, Kate. Thank goodness I was able to help you get out of that entanglement. I never understood how, with the frightful example of our parents' married life, you could contemplate marrying at all, except, perhaps, as a way of escape from our awful home life. But that's a coward's way out and asking for more trouble."

"I wasn't using Mark as an escape. It would have been insulting to him to do so. I was fond of him and still am. We were good friends."

"Well, I've no time now to go raking over that old ground, but if you take my advice, you'll let that connection die and concentrate on the present and a decent career and freedom. I don't imagine that Mark will be all that pleased to renew the acquaintance, either. Men are so vain. To be thrown over is a sad jolt to their egos. A salutary experience for his lordship. He was always too arrogant for me. You had a lucky escape. He would quite likely have developed into just such a domineering brute as our unlamented father."

Pamela's face was hard and cold. The damage which their father had done to their home life still lived on, thought Kate, for he had imbued in his eldest daughter a bitter dislike of men and had turned her into an unrelenting feminist, bent on looking after herself at all costs. She wondered how Pamela viewed her employer, whom she had only lately taken to addressing by his Christian name. He was a successful member of parliament, aiming for high office, and apparently taking Pamela with him, for she worked indefatigably for him, and seemed to have no other life outside her job.

"You and Mark never hit it off. I shall always be grateful to him for his friendship and support through those wretched years."

"You're too soft, Kate, as our mother was. In fact, I was surprised, as well as delighted, that you managed to break free. Mark Vermont always had you in his pocket. How did he take it, by the way? You've never said much about it."

"Our own business."

"Well, I think you'd be very ill advised now to accept this

invitation from the Vermonts. The past is dead. Think of the future. And let me have your letter of application for this job on Monday, Kate. It really will be a splendid opportunity for you,'' concluded Pamela, drawing on her gloves.

"I'll think about it," said Kate, handing her sister the red umbrella.

Registering Kate's dry tone, Pamela paused at the door and her expression softened a little as she said,

"I'm only thinking of your good, you know."

Words, thought Kate, calculated to send a shiver down anybody's spine.

She stood by the window and watched her sister drive off in her little grey car. Pamela, at twenty-eight, was assured, successful and single-minded, but it sometimes seemed to Kate that somewhere on the way, her heart had been mislaid. She had always had a bossy nature, which Kate, four years her junior, had learned to live with, but there had once been more warmth there. She remembered one winter's day, it had been Pamela's seventeenth birthday, after a searing family row, when her sister had turned on her as soon as they were alone, her face flaming with passion. She could hear the words now.

"No man is ever going to run my life. I'm getting out of here. I'll make my own way and be free." And within a month, she had gone.

The rain was easing up, and a small patch of blue sky appeared. Restless, turning over the questions Pamela had raised in her mind, feeling the small flat like a prison around her, she decided to take her problems into the Surrey hills.

It was well past lunchtime when she started along the footpath through the woods which she and Valerie had followed so many times when they were in their teens, for it led to the top of a hill which had been their favourite place for picnics. The fallen leaves of autumn were wet and spongy under her feet, and the air was full of the bitter-sweet tang of the dying year. She breathed it in deeply, relishing it after the foetid, petrol-laden air of London streets, and took an apple from her shoulder bag as she stepped out. A fitful sun lightened the scene, and in spite of the lateness of the season, there was still plenty of colour around her. Tawny brown bracken lined the path, a gorse bush sported a few golden flowers, and patches of emerald green moss shone out among faded heather and jostling pine seedlings. Birch trees carried a few wisps of late foliage and scattered holly trees bore copious berries.

It took her an hour to reach the top of the hill, and there she sat on a fallen tree trunk and took out the modest packet of cheese and biscuits which she had stowed in her raincoat pocket. The sun emerged from a bank of cloud into a large blue expanse, and just then it felt like summer again as she looked across the wide expanse of the weald stretched before her to the faint line of the South Downs in the distance.

Reviewing the unsettling discussion with her sister, she wondered whether Mark would indeed resent her presence if she accepted the invitation for Christmas. She had not seen or heard from him since she had broken off their engagement, but there had been no angry recriminations at their parting. That was not Mark's way. Incredulity on his part had given way to a demand for a fuller explanation, which she had been unable to give. There had been so many strands in her wish to break free. Her mother's faltering words as she lay dying, begging her never to marry. The very fact that she had known Mark for so long, had looked up to him in some awe as her best friend's brother when she was twelve years old to his eighteen, and had been dominated by him as she grew up and their friendship ripened, seemed to preclude the element of romance which she felt was lacking. And rebellion against his domination grew as time passed and the difference in their ages counted for less. He simply took her for granted. Annexed her. She remembered Pamela's acid remark one day when observing Mark charming an attractive young woman at Evelyn Vermont's wedding. "You for domestic utility, Kate. Others for fun." It was not an entirely implausible accusation, for although at all times Mark had been kind to her, their relationship was on too mundane a level, she felt. Made so, perhaps, because he had known her since childhood. The magic was missing.

An Invitation

And that brought her to the third strand, Philippe Touraine, where magic certainly did remain like a silver wand from the past. Even now, the prospect of seeing him again caused her pulse to quicken. She had been so much in love with him at sixteen. At that last meeting with Mark, she had wondered for a moment whether he had known of that secret adolescent passion, for he had taken her by the shoulders when he had asked if there was anybody else and had searched her face as she denied it. "Are you quite sure, Kate?" he had asked. And she had refused to admit to herself that the girlhood involvement had any validity six years later, and had given him another decisive no. But somewhere in her heart, she felt, the comparison between Philippe's sparkling personality and Mark's matter-of-fact way with her had always been there to Mark's disadvantage. And in the end Mark had accepted her decision with a grim face that revealed little and had left her, striding away across the field from their rendezvous without a backward glance. And she had felt her knees buckle and had sunk, exhausted and drained, to the grass, leaning against the stile for support.

The sun was sinking now and the air felt suddenly cold as she took out Valerie's letter and read it again " . . . we can all be easy together as before. I know Mark will welcome you as we all will." Perhaps, thought Kate. Perhaps. But she suddenly longed to see her old friends, feel the warmth of their affection. Surely the interval had been long enough for wounded feelings to heal, for a fresh start to be made. She would accept the invitation and look forward to Christmas at Greenhurst.

The sun now appeared as a small orange ball above a grey belt of mist on the horizon instead of the golden glow that had bathed her in its warmth for the past half hour, and she felt cold. It was time to be gone. Mist now hovered around the footpath, colours were muted as though covered by a blue-grey veil, and from summer to winter had taken only a few minutes. She lengthened her stride down the hill, but her usually observant eyes saw little of her surroundings, her mind being occupied just then with two faces from the past:

the dark, lively face of Philippe Touraine and the more mature, rugged countenance of Mark Vermont. The first love of her life, nurtured only on dreams for the past eight years but still lingering on, and the broken engagement, rooted in reality but lacking in romance. It should be an interesting Christmas.

2
Christmas Eve

Greenhurst was a solidly built grey stone house on the edge of Cheryton village. The houses in the tree-lined road became progressively larger, starting with cottages at the end nearest to the heath and finishing with imposing residences at the far end. Kate eyed her old home curiously as she went by. It was one of the cottages, undistinguished, and rendered less attractive by the cheap garage built on to it, which was all her father had been able to afford. She hoped that it was a happier home now, and shivered in the cold east wind as she hurried past. Greenhurst was three quarters of the way down the road, neither imposing nor poky, just comfortable and roomy, and Kate greeted the holly tree leaning at a rather drunken angle by the front gate like an old friend. Before she could grasp the knocker on the wide oak door, it opened and Valerie stood there, smiling, her hands outstretched.

"Kate, I meant to meet the train at Ellarton, but Dad forgot I'd booked the car and disappeared with it after lunch and hasn't been seen since. I'm so sorry. Here, give me your case."

"A bus was waiting. No trouble."

"Oh, it's good to see you."

"Indeed it is," said Mrs. Vermont, coming into the hall. "It's been too long, dear."

And Kate, yielding to her warm embrace, felt that she had come home. With tea and buttered toast waiting for her in the sitting-room, she sank down into a capacious armchair by the side of a blazing fire and looked round her with pleasure. Nothing had changed. The faded old rose carpet, the chintz-covered chairs, even the bowls of hyacinths which were distributed round the large bay window sill and filled the air with their fragrance were as she remembered them at past Christmases. And any fears that breaking off her engagement to Mark would have cast a shadow over her relationship with his family were laid to rest, for Valerie and her mother, and later her elder sister, Evelyn, welcomed her with the old easy affection, as though nothing had changed and her two years' absence had been of no more significance than a long holiday away from them. But the crunch would come, she thought, when she had to face Mark, not due until the next morning.

"Mark couldn't get away today. He's so busy nowadays. Having to take over as Director of the Station so unexpectedly, and move from his flat in Deanswood to the Director's house at the Station and help Dr. Brynton's widow find another home, has just about taken over every spare moment he's got, I think. We've scarcely seen him these last months," said Valerie later that evening as she and Kate put the finishing touches to the Christmas tree standing in the hall.

"I thought Dr. Brynton's second in command was a man called Wicklow."

"Yes, but he left to take up another appointment over a year ago, so Mark was next in line. Not that he rejoices about that. He thought a great deal of Darrel Brynton, as you know, and both the Bryntons became very close friends after Wicklow left. Mark was very shocked and distressed at the loss, I think, although he never lets on a great deal. He seemed very bitter about it, though, when he told us. Some fool of a motorist who'd had too much to drink was the cause of the accident. And Jean Brynton was completely broken up. Mark's been doing his best to help her, I gather."

"He would be good at that," said Kate, remembering the worst times at her home when Mark's support had helped her so much. Not overt sympathy, but a firm hand there all the time.

"M'm. He didn't want her to leave her home until she'd

recovered a bit, but Little Fenton, that's the house in the grounds of Fenton Grange Horticultural Station, is the official residence of the Director, and Jean wanted to move out quickly. It had become haunted for her, she said. Anyway, he's bringing her with him tomorrow, and her little girl, Diana, and when he telephoned Mother last night, he asked her to see that nobody mentioned anything about her loss in Jean's presence. She's apt to dissolve into tears. It will help her if we behave as though we don't know anything about it. He thinks that as we're all strangers, it will make things easier for her. She's avoiding her friends because sympathy undoes her.''

"I can understand that. Anyway, we can try to make it a happy Christmas for the little girl,'' said Kate, hanging a gaily wrapped parcel labelled Diana on a low branch of the tree.

"Yes. It's a good thing Philippe's coming. He always livens things up.''

"Are they all coming? The Touraine branch of the family?''

"No. Only Philippe and Madeleine. Philippe's landed a part in a T.V. soap opera here. Starts work immediately after Christmas. Madeleine's been spending the week in London with him and is going back next week. They promised Aunt Hester that they'd visit us while they were here. She and Uncle Henri, believe it or not, have gone on a Christmas cruise to the Canaries. The first Christmas they've spent away from the farm in living memory.''

"Philippe may well prove very successful on the T.V. screen. He has such a sparkling personality. That is, unless it's dimmed very much since I last saw him, which is admittedly a long time ago.''

"Nothing will ever dim Philippe. I sometimes find him a bit tiring. You don't always want sparkle. For a party, though, he's as good as champagne and a fine antidote to Hugh,'' concluded Valerie with mischief in her eyes.

"Let's not be nasty about Hugh,'' they chorused in union, echoing the old family joke.

Kate shook her head, smiling, for Evelyn's husband had

never fitted in well with the Vermont family and Mrs. Vermont had often to chide her irreverent children for their attitude to him.

"He's a good husband and father, I'm sure, and that, as my sister Pamela would say, is as rare as water in the desert."

"For all that, I can't think why Evelyn chose him. His prim, fussy little ways would drive me mad. It seems to work, though, and that's all that matters. How is Pamela, by the way?"

"Flying high in the wake of her M.P. I haven't seen her lately because I'm in the dog-house for not applying for a marvellous job her chief could have got for me. She can't understand my lack of ambition," concluded Kate drily.

"I couldn't work in London. Not my scene at all. I never thought it was yours either."

"I've never felt at home there, but I needed to get away after that last fraught year. Do you think we've overdone the tinsel?" she added, eyeing the glittering tree.

"Can't overdo tinsel where children are concerned. Anyway, I'm glad you've come back to us."

Kate gave her friend a warm smile and thought how appealing she looked in the cherry red skirt and sweater, trailing a piece of tinsel in her hand. Her fair hair, hanging straight to her shoulders, shone like silk in the lamplight, framing an oval face with sensitive features and delphinium blue eyes. Of the two distinct strains that made up the Vermont family, the gentle artistic strain of the father and the practical, managing strain of the mother, Valerie had inherited the former, while Mark and Evelyn reflected much of their mother's character. They were an unusually united family, and for that Kate had always envied them.

"I shall shortly be out of work," went on Valerie airily. "The *Ellarton Gazette* is folding next month, pushed out by that rival rag, the *Clarion*."

"Oh, Val. I'm sorry."

"I'm not particularly. Advertisement layouts can pall, and although I'm sorry for the rest of the staff, I've been thinking of a change. Trouble is, I don't quite know what sort of a job I'd like. My qualifications don't seem to fit me for earning a living. I can draw a bit, paint a bit, do dried flower pictures, and I'm quite good at lettering. Who would want to pay me for that, although that's what I enjoy doing?''

"You under-rate your artistic talent."

"It's not good enough to earn me a living, although I did sell a couple of my dried flower pictures to an arty-crafty shop in Dilford last month. And that reminds me. This is your Christmas present. It's too heavy to put on the tree,'' she said, fishing out a framed picture from behind the oak chest. "Sorry it's not wrapped. With my love, Kate."

Kate looked with delight at the elegant bouquet of dried, pressed flowers behind glass. She had long admired her friend's skill in this sphere and in the past had helped her search for material in gardens and countryside. This was a collection of wild flowers; celandine, stitchwort, red campion, dog-rose, cranesbill, harebell and rosebay, all with their colours beautifully preserved.

"I thought it would remind you of our walks and the Surrey countryside while you're submerged in London," added Valerie, brushing aside Kate's warm thanks with a smile.

When Kate went up to bed, she was feeling happily reassured by her welcome back to this family which she held in such affection, but she still had the biggest hurdle to face in meeting Mark again. He was a man used to dictating the course his life would follow, and to have been blown off it by a girl he had taken charge of since her schooldays was tantamount to a totally unexpected mutiny in the ranks.

Seated at the dressing-table, brushing her hair, she felt that she had been in limbo during the past two years. The cold cruelty of her father had seemed to grow worse during the last few months before a heart attack had killed him, and her mother's release from his tryanny had come too late, for she had suffered a long and painful illness, and had died barely nine months after her husband's death. Kate had nursed her to the end, passionately wishing to make up to her for her ruined life, and had emerged from this morass of

A Slender Thread

sorrow and suffering in a pulpy state, wishing only to escape to some neutral zone, disentangle herself from an engagement that lacked all romance and remain free from emotional involvements. She had needed desperately that breathing space, and knew that she had, as it were, firmed up during the interval, could stand on her own feet. And she had every intention of remaining independent.

She put down the hair brush and studied the face reflected in the mirror with calm objectivity. A serious face, with smooth chestnut hair curving round her cheeks, slate grey eyes, straight nose, too wide a mouth. It looked a little grim now, as though squaring up for a fight, and she smiled as she turned away. It was Christmas Eve, she was back with her friends, her own woman, and it was foolish to feel nervous about meeting that male chauvinist to whom she had once been engaged. They could be friends, she hoped. That was all.

She went to the window and drew back the curtain to look out across the fields to the dark line of the Surrey hills. The moon had not yet risen and myriads of stars glittered in the dark sky. She could see the church spire of the village, and beyond that the occasional flash of cars on the main road, but only the call of an owl broke the silence of the night. Christmas Eve. A magical time. Serenity stole over her. Not a time for thinking of past bitterness. She remained there for some minutes until the cold drove her to bed.

3
The Old Magic

However Kate had visualised this first meeting with Mark after two years had passed since their broken engagement, she had never expected it to pass off as though nothing had changed between them, but that, in fact, was what happened.

She saw the car draw up to the porch while she was watering a cyclamen plant on the dining-room window sill, and felt a little annoyed with herself for the quickening of her pulse and a feeling not far off panic as he emerged, tall and broad-shouldered, wearing a sheepskin jacket over tweed trousers, his black hair blowing in the east wind as he helped out a slender woman with tawny coloured hair who was carrying a sheaf of flowers. Then he lifted out a little girl in a red coat and red woolly hat, pale grey woollen stockings and miniature red Wellington boots, who looked a little scared as she took her mother's hand.

Kate hung back, letting the family welcome them in the hall before she joined them, and Mark turned and saw her.

"Hullo, Kate. It's good to see you," he said calmly, and putting a hand on each of her shoulders, subjected her to a thoughtful scrutiny. "Let me see what London has done to you. Paler, but a little more flesh on your bones. Otherwise, in good working order, I'd say. A happy Christmas, my dear," he concluded, and kissed her before releasing her and introducing her to Jean Brynton.

Masking her confused annoyance at his proprietorial air

and the amused look in his eyes as he released her which told her that he had sensed her confusion, she turned to his companion, and was immediately aware of a bruised spirit that drew her sympathy. She had lived too long with deep unhappiness in her old home not to recognise the signs, although Jean Brynton's face was smiling as she returned Kate's greeting. She was very pale, with an almost transparent look of fragility, a sensitive mouth and large browny-gold eyes curiously dull, with dark shadows beneath them. It was difficult to judge her age, for the face had a shut-away expression and there was no vitality there, but Kate guessed her to be in the mid thirties. Her little daughter had been drawn to the Christmas tree at the back of the hall, and stood before it, wide-eyed and entranced, and Kate was glad that they had festooned it with so much tinsel. Then Mrs. Vermont was ushering her guests upstairs and Kate seized the opportunity to return the watering can to the greenhouse and gain a little breathing space, for meeting Mark again had disturbed her composure.

In the sanctuary of the greenhouse, she found Mark's father brooding over a wilting white cyclamen.

"My only failure with cyclamen this year. Some grubs must be eating the roots," he said, then gave her a sheepish smile. "Have they arrived, our French relatives?"

"Not yet. But Mark and Mrs. Brynton have."

"Oh good. I must come in, or I shall be in the dog-house. I'm no good at these social occasions, you know," he said confidentially.

"I do know," said Kate, laughing, for Mr. Vermont's failings in that respect had always been born with resignation but not without comment by his family.

Kate had a specially soft spot in her heart for this tall, thin, stooping man, with his long, lugubrious face, straggly grey hair and gentle, absent-minded manner, which was deceptive, for Roland Vermont was a very percipient man in his own way, and the members of his family maintained that the absent-minded manner was an escapist ploy. He had been a successful commercial artist, but had retired five years ago, and now divided his time between the greenhouse, fishing and pottering round the country, drawing old churches and any odd corners that appealed to him. And it was from her father that Valerie had inherited her artistic talent.

As he stood mourning over the white cyclamen, Kate took his arm and said consolingly, "Think of the beauties you've raised for the house. You can spare this Christmas present for the grubs."

He patted her hand and they went back to the house together, and were welcomed by a delicious smell of coffee.

A little later, enticed by the sun which had emerged to temper the east wind, the younger members of the party went off for a walk on the heath, leaving Evelyn to help her mother in the kitchen. With Mark, Jean Brynton and Valerie ahead, Kate found herself paired off with Evelyn's husband, Hugh, and their son Jeremy, a sturdy, sandy-haired little boy who was casting rather suspicious glances at Diana as they walked along. Fortunately, the family dog, a shaggy old sheepdog named Crusoe, was breaking the ice and forming a link between them.

"Country air must be welcome again after London, Kate," observed Hugh.

"Yes, even with an east wind keener than I'm used to," replied Kate, turning up the collar of her tweed coat as an icy gust assailed her.

"It'll be better coming back. Jeremy, watch what you're doing," he added as his son, jumping up and down on the icy surface of a puddle in an effort to break it, skidded and almost knocked his small companion over.

The sandy path led through heather and gorse and round birch trees whose filigree tracery stood out blackly above their silver trunks against the pale blue sky. They were making for the pond, and Kate, who had known every inch of the heath from her earliest days, responded politely to Hugh's discourse on the bird-life in his garden while her eyes greeted like old friends familiar trees, vistas, old picnic sites. Hugh's thin, precise voice somehow robbed anything he had to say of interest, and she had never been able to feel

A Slender Thread

at ease with him. He was always so formal, even with those nearest him. His thin face seemed almost over-burdened by the heavy horn-rimmed spectacles, and his face seldom betrayed any emotion. He worked for the Inland Revenue in the neighbouring town of Ellarton and Kate wondered whether bureaucracy had petrified him. He was, however, endlessly patient with his son, answering his multitudinous questions always with care and grave attention, a virtue demonstrated once more when they arrived at the pond, and the presence of swans and ducks drew many queries from both Diana and Jeremy.

On the way back, Kate found herself alone with Mark, well ahead of the rest of the party.

"Are you happy in London, Kate?" he asked.

"Neither happy nor unhappy," she replied after a little thought. "My job is pleasant enough. No serious complaints, anyway, but I miss the country."

"Do you see much of Pamela?"

"Not a great deal. She keeps an eye on me, but she's a busy and important person now, attached to an even more important high-flyer, and I fear I disappoint her in my lack of drive, as she puts it."

He smiled at her dry tone and said, "I'm glad she hasn't infected you with her own brand of aggressive ambition."

"Did you think she would?"

"She's a very embittered, strong-willed woman, your sister. I think perhaps you've allowed her to influence you too much in the past."

"She had a lot to make her bitter."

"So did you. And she walked out and left you to shoulder it all and care for your mother in her illness after your father died."

"Well, it's past history now. And I had your family to help me. I shall always be grateful for that, Mark. In spite of what happened," she faltered.

He gave her a swift glance.

"You know, when you first saw me this morning, you looked as guilty as hell. Is that what kept you away?"

"Yes."

"How foolish! Even divorced people remain friends, you know, and we've known each other too many years to be anything else."

Kate looked at him a little warily, hearing again Pamela's words. Mark Vermont always had you in his pocket. She decided to change the subject.

"I'm looking forward to seeing Philippe and his sister again. A reminder of those lovely holidays in Normandy. I wonder if they've changed much in eight years. Have you seen them lately, Mark?"

"About a year ago we had a family get-together over there to celebrate our aunt and uncle's silver wedding anniversary at which Philippe put in a brief appearance. Madeleine doesn't grow any less reserved with maturity, but I don't doubt that you'll find Philippe's charm as romantically appealing as ever."

These disconcerting words were spoken amiably enough, but glancing at him quickly, she was aware of an amused irony that nettled her and she replied coolly, "Could be."

He laughed and took her arm.

"Don't be cross, Kate. Most of us go through a moonstruck phase of calf love, and the memory lingers on."

"Your imagination was more active in those days than I realised," she said, freeing her arm.

"Come off it, my dear. That starry expression in your eyes at the mere mention of Philippe's name at that time could hardly be missed. But you were sixteen then, and what more natural? I remember a few lunacies of my own at that age."

"One with red hair, I remember. Valerie and I were at the giggly stage and had fits about it."

"Yes. What was her name? Rachel. That was it. But, unlike you, I didn't worship from afar and so my disillusionment came swiftly."

"Cynic."

"Realist. You're better at fencing than you used to be."

Maybe, she thought, but she knew who was even better,

A Slender Thread

and giving him a little smile, she ran ahead after Crusoe, who had galloped past them trailing a woollen scarf, pursued by the children.

A rakish little red sports car was parked in the drive behind Mark's car when they arrived back, and in the hall Philippe and his sister were just unburdening themselves of coats and scarves. From the mêlée of introductions and greetings, Philippe emerged to take both of Kate's hands, kiss her and say with a flashing smile, "My old playmate. I was delighted to learn that you would be with us. How long is it?"

"Nearly eight years."

"Too long. But it only seems like yesterday. Come and tell me what you've been doing since then."

"You'll have more to tell me, Philippe. My life will sound very dull beside the glamour and success of yours. It *is* good to see you," she added, smiling up at him as he took her coat, threw it on the oak chest, put an arm round her shoulders and drew her to the fire in the sitting-room.

He had changed surprisingly little, she thought, as they brought each other up to date. The black hair a little less unruly, the dark eyes as lively as ever, the ready tongue and lurking smile as charming now in the man as they were in the boy, with the added assurance that success had brought. Both he and his sister took after their English mother in looks, and both were bilingual, as at home in their mother's tongue as their father's, but Madeleine was as reserved and withdrawn as her brother was dynamic, and to Kate she had remained a stranger. Her fondness for her brother, however, had never been in doubt.

"I've been lucky," he said. "Spent a fruitful two years in American television. A friend got me the right introductions. The experience was valuable, and made me known over there. Now I've got into a series on television here and hope it will launch me on this side of the Channel because I'd like to settle in England."

"We shall be following your career, applauding your success."

"Now that I've found you again, we mustn't lose touch,

Kate. I'm thinking of taking a flat in London as a base. Madeleine would like to join me. Find a part-time job herself, perhaps, and housekeep for me, and act as my agent. She's had a bit of experience at that." He stooped to pat Crusoe's shaggy head. "What fun we had together when we were kids, you and I, Kate. Remember?"

"As if I could forget."

"And we can again. You haven't changed, except that you're better looking. The coltish angles gone, the features firmed up and just as endearing," he added with a smile, his head on one side as he considered her.

"You've changed, in that you never used to flatter."

"Not flattery. Just the facts. Without you, the holidays would have been deadly. Life on the farm was never my scene."

They were still reminiscing together when they were all called to the dining-room where the turkey was waiting.

When Kate looked back at that Christmas party, she saw it as an inexorable slide down to the feet of Philippe Touraine, conquered by his lively charm as she had been in her teens, with odd, disconcerting bumps on the way, resulting in a breathless, shaken up state of mind. The slide started in the afternoon, when Philippe organised charades ostensibly to amuse the children, but enjoying himself hugely in the process. Acting out one word by partnering her in an exaggeratedly passionate tango, entering into it with zest, Philippe with a makeshift sombrero on his head, Kate with a fringed shawl and a flower in her hair, she was not prepared for the shattering effect of his close embrace. Glued together as one, they swayed and dipped and glided, and Kate felt as though her bones were melting. His cheek against hers, she closed her eyes and the slide was well under way. His dancing eyes when he released her told her that he was well aware of that fact.

The first bump came when she went out to the kitchen, having volunteered for tea-duty to recover her equilibrium a little. Passing the dining-room, she saw someone standing by the window gazing out. It was dusk, but she recognised Jean Brynton's slender back silhouetted against the darkening sky. She was standing with shoulders hunched, arms crossed, hugging herself tightly as though afraid that she might fall to pieces. The impression was of such lonely desolation against the sound of chatter and laughter from the sitting-room that Kate's mood of euphoria received a sudden jolt and her heart ached for this bereaved stranger. She hesitated, suspecting tears, wondering whether she would do more harm than good by intruding if Jean Brynton had escaped there to collect herself. Then, trusting to her instinct, she crossed the room, put a gentle hand on Jean's shoulder and said softly, "Jean, would you like to give me a hand with the tea?"

"Oh, yes, of course. A big party to cater for."

Her voice was a little shaky, and in the light of the kitchen her face was sheet white and her eyes narrowed with pain. But she spoke cheerfully enough as they busied themselves, although at what cost Kate could only guess.

Evelyn joined them just as they were loading up two tea trolleys.

"We thought we'd transfer it all to the two tables we've set up in the sitting-room so that people can help themselves. Don't suppose anyone will want much more than a piece of Christmas cake, but you never know with kids. Jeremy has an insatiable appetite," said Evelyn.

"Diana can hold her own, too," said Jean. "I'll try to steer her clear of the jam tarts, for which she has a passion, as tarts seem always to finish up jam side down on the carpet."

"We don't worry about little things like that," said Evelyn airily with a smile that transformed her into a young edition of her mother.

At thirty-two, the eldest of the Vermont children, Evelyn Vermont tended to the buxom, with dark hair and a fresh complexion, and had the same good-natured, easy-going temperament as her mother. To Kate's enjoyment, she managed her husband with equal skill, too, although needing a different technique to cope blandly with Hugh's irresistible itch to put everyone right, an itch which drove less benign natures to impotent fury, and tested them on this occasion when he joined them in the kitchen and cast critical eyes over the trolleys.

"Want any help?" he asked, frowning slightly.

"No thanks, dear. All organised," said Evelyn.

"Haven't you any wholemeal bread and butter? Much better for the children than that white stuff."

"Didn't think of it," said Kate, who was rather pleased with her jam sandwiches for the children.

"Yes, there's a wholemeal loaf here," said Hugh, opening the bread-bin. "I'll make a few more."

"You do that, dear," said Evelyn. "We'll take this lot in or the tea will get cold."

They left him meticulously applying the thinnest scraping of butter on to the brown bread, fat being one item in his long list of undesirable foods in the battle to keep fit.

Indulging in a treasure hunt before the children went to bed, Philippe caught Kate alone in the lobby at the back of the house where Wellington boots, old coats and scarves, and fishing tackle were housed.

"This looks a likely place," she said, searching inside a Wellington boot.

"And mistletoe, too, as if we need encouraging," said Philippe, taking her in his arms and kissing her. This he performed in such a lingering, expert way that she was left breathless and trembling when he released her.

"You've had a lot of practice since we last met," she said, smiling at him.

"I don't know why I didn't start earlier with you. Sweet sixteen was, after all, a ripe enough time and I believe you were rather fond of me. Yes?"

"Sixteen is a very susceptible age," she said lightly.

"Confess now," he said, taking her in his arms again, his eyes sparkling as he ran a caressing finger down her cheek.

"You brought so much laughter and fun into my life on those holidays, Philippe. How could I not fall in love with such a charming scamp? I thought it was a secret, though. You never gave any sign of suspecting it. I see now that you did but had your mind set on more sophisticated girls than one gauche sixteen-year-old."

A Slender Thread

"If I'd had any sense, I'd have appreciated the old-fashioned innocence, but towards the end I became a bit embroiled with the family, restless, wanting to escape. Anyway, I appreciate it now," he added, and kissed her with more urgency.

"Break it up," said Mark's crisp voice. "The treasure's been found and my father, bless his soul, is going to perform some conjuring tricks for the kids, for which purpose he needs a fishing rod. Don't ask me why."

Philippe, no whit put out of his stride, said affably, "Well, we mustn't miss that. Never a dull moment. Come along, Kate."

Taking her arm, he returned her to the party, leaving Mark to follow with the fishing rod. Kate, flushed and in a confused state of euphoria, nevertheless wished that Mark had not witnessed that embrace. A quite illogical reaction of guilt which she dismissed as absurd after a few moments' reflection.

During the dancing that followed the children's departure for bed, Philippe monopolised her. He was a good dancer and they were well matched. It was while he was twisting her round with laughing abandon that she received another jolt to her starry mood when she caught Madeleine Touraine studying her with a venomous expression that chilled her as effectively as a bucket of cold water. In a moment, as she caught Kate's eye, Madeleine's face became expressionless and she turned with some remark to Mrs. Vermont beside her. Kate, dancing on, was puzzled by this degree of hostility. When she had visited them as a schoolgirl, Madeleine, five years older than her brother, had remained a shadowy figure, cool and reserved, too old to join in their escapades, and Kate had never really got to know her at all. Resembling Philippe in looks, with the same regular features and dark colouring, but quite lacking his liveliness and charm, his sister gave an impression of austerity, with her smooth black hair moulded to her head and taken back from her face with a clean-cut ballerina effect.

"Anything wrong?" asked Philippe, holding her close.

"Not a thing," she said, and dismissed the incident.

They finished up singing songs, with Jean playing for them, ranging geographically from 'Sur le Pont d'Avignon' to 'Over the Sea to Skye', with a few old camp-fire songs thrown in.

It was nearly midnight when Philippe and Madeleine left. He had asked Kate for the address and telephone number of her flat.

"I'll be in touch," he had whispered as he kissed her goodbye before taking his leave of the others.

"I don't know how you all feel," said Evelyn, closing the front door, "but I'm going to make a pot of tea."

Hugh winced slightly and said,

"Isn't it a bit late for that, dear? It'll keep you awake."

"Not a chance," said Evelyn cheerfully. "I'm parched and exhausted. Does anybody else find Philippe exhausting? All that verve!"

And so they finished the evening sitting round in varying states of exhaustion, drinking tea and listening to Jean playing soothing music to them. She was a good pianist and had seemed glad to spend so much time that evening at the piano.

From her fireside chair, Kate, still in a state of bemusement, looked round the family circle with affectionate eyes. It had been a lovely Christmas Day, and she felt a warm glow of happiness at being back again, part of this family to which she had always been so attached. Her eyes rested on Mark across the room. He was lounging back on the sofa, long legs stretched before him, his eyes half closed, apparently lulled, or perhaps absorbed, by the lilting serenity of 'Clair de Lune'. Studying that familiar face, it occurred to her then that he looked tired, lines etched across his forehead which she did not remember before, the face leaner, a little gaunt. The death of his friend and his unexpectedly early succession to the directorship of the Horticultural Station must have imposed considerable strain on him, and her heart warmed to him in sympathy. How childish to be on the defensive with him that morning, seeing his friendship as a threat to her freedom, suspecting that he was putting her in his pocket again. That was what came of

A Slender Thread

listening to Pamela. Of course they would remain friends, affectionate friends as they had always been. Thus when he looked up and caught her scrutiny, he was rewarded with a warm smile from her which he acknowledged with a little nod and a faint twitch of his mouth as though he had read her thoughts and was confirming that all was well between them.

4
Family Circle

In the garden below, frost trimmed every blade of grass and leaf, and ice glittered in the bird bath under a cloudless, pale blue sky. Kate stood at her bedroom window and gazed at this fairy-like aspect with pleasure. The keen east wind of Christmas Day had dropped, and the world was silent and still, as though caught in a trance. Then Crusoe came ambling round the summer-house, his large shaggy paws leaving prints across the frosty lawn.

These somewhat arctic conditions in no way deterred the head of the household, who declared at the breakfast table that he would be spending the day fishing.

"It's far too cold, Roland," protested his wife. "You'll get pleurisy."

"The sun will soon warm things up, my dear."

"Well, don't stay long. And do wrap up warmly."

"Of course. A turkey sandwich and a piece of cheese will do me nicely."

"You're not going all day!" exclaimed his wife.

Mark, who was obviously a slow starter, not at his brightest at the breakfast table, merely lifted his eyes to heaven and proceeded to eat his toast and marmalade while the rest of the family took sides. It would do no good, thought Kate, for Roland Vermont, with his sweet, vague manner, went his own way when he chose, and that morning was no exception.

"We'll come along with you this morning," said Hugh. "I'd like to be able to show Jeremy a kingfisher."

A Slender Thread

Roland Vermont's hastily concealed look of dismay suggested to Kate that it was not so much the joy of fishing as the desire for an interlude of solitude that had made him so determined, and the amused gleam in Mark's eyes as he passed her the marmalade suggested that the thought had also occurred to him.

But to the river they all went, Roland muffled up at his wife's insistence like the Michelin man. If solitude was his aim, however, he achieved it, for the others found it too cold to linger and went for a walk along the river bank, leaving him huddled up on the bank surrounded by fishing paraphernalia.

Finding herself paired with Jean, Kate discovered that they shared a love for poetry when Jean quoted,

"To smell the thrilling-sweet and rotten
 Unforgettable, unforgotten
 River smell."

"Rupert Brooke," said Kate. "Rather belittled now, but I've always liked his work."

And soon they were in a deep discussion of poetry until Jean said, "Truth expressed with beautiful economy can be too piercing sometimes. I can hardly bear to read Thomas Hardy now." And then, fearing that she had betrayed too much, she went on lightly, "It's good to see Jeremy and Diana get on so happily together. An only child can be very lonely. I was one myself. I think they've spotted that elusive kingfisher. We'd better freeze."

They stayed still while Hugh, on bended knee, held the children close and pointed ahead. To Jean and Kate, the bird was hidden, but after a moment or two they saw the flash of blue and bronze as the kingfisher took wing down the river and vanished round a bend.

"And there," said Valerie, joining the ornithological party, "is a bullfinch. On that bramble, Jeremy."

"No, it's a cock chaffinch," corrected Hugh. "The bullfinch has a black crown, not blue, and doesn't have those white wing bars."

This making the third time Valerie had been put right on that walk, she fell back to join Mark and Kate.

Family Circle

"How Evelyn stays so good tempered living with that know-all, I don't know," she declared.

"Hugh's all right," said Mark. "If you got your facts right, you wouldn't be corrected."

"Well, it's very irritating."

"You want to try to catch him out."

"That will be the day. Have you ever managed it?"

"Once or twice," said Mark with a little smile. "On matters horticultural."

"Well, I find his company deadly. I wish Philippe had been able to stay longer. He offsets Hugh."

"He is a professional entertainer," said Mark drily.

"And Kate was his leading lady yesterday. Did you enjoy our dazzling cousin's attentions, Kate?" asked Valerie.

"Very much."

"I didn't think you could have measles twice," observed Mark, and Valerie went into peals of laughter which nettled Kate somewhat.

"We always hit it off well together, Phil and I."

"As long as you don't take our cousin too seriously. Nobody should take Philippe seriously," said Valerie.

"You're growing up, Val," said her brother approvingly.

"What a needling pair you are! Philippe always was, and still is, a delightful person," said Kate.

"No need to get so ruffled," said Mark calmly. "After all, we've known him longer than you and are not so easily dazzled."

"He was a horrible little boy. Always slid out of trouble and others got the blame. The biggest slice of cake somehow always went Phil's way," said Valerie.

"That's not the way I remember him," said Kate, trying to keep cool under Mark's amused scrutiny.

"You only knew the holiday version, my dear. One thing I will predict. He'll be a big hit in this soap opera on television. Before long, he'll be getting trunks of fan mail. And won't that please him!" said Mark.

"Of course. It would please anybody. A proof of success," said Kate.

"And a boost to an ego that certainly doesn't need it.

37

A Slender Thread

Don't mind us, Kate. We're only teasing. And giving a little warning," said Valerie.

"Unnecessary," said Kate briskly.

"A second go of measles might be more serious," said Mark.

"I can be considered old enough to look after myself," replied Kate sweetly.

"I've never thought you a very good judge of character, my dear."

"Is that why I became engaged to you?"

At this riposte, Mark laughed and tweaked her hair.

"I left myself right open to that, didn't I? I plead a good many more years experience than either of you two children, and I'd sooner plump for old Hugh in a tight corner than our charming cousin."

And Kate, who remembered from the old days how fighting with Mark was like trying to dent a cushion, throttled back her anger and turned with some relief to Diana, who was lagging behind the advance party, her doll trailing from one hand, looking a little tired. Under the red woolly hat her face was pale, but she gave Kate a tentative smile in response to her greeting, her dark blue, long-lashed eyes searching Kate's face as though trying to identify her among all these strangers.

"Hullo," said Kate. "That's a very pretty doll. What's her name?"

"Pulsatilla," replied Diana, enunciating carefully.

"There speaks a botanist's daughter," said Mark, laughing. "Would you like a lift? Auntie Kate will carry Pulsatilla for you."

Diana nodded eagerly, handed Kate the doll and lifted her arms, whereupon Mark swung her up on his shoulders, holding her hands and carrying her jockey fashion for the rest of the way back.

Walking behind with Valerie, Kate wondered whether Mark's easy acceptance of her as no more than a friend now owed much to a new channel for his affections in Jean and her little daughter. They were all three on such obviously close terms. She ought to feel glad if that were so, for it would relieve her sense of guilt, put at rest any suspicion that he was aiming to put her in his pocket again, and enable her to enjoy his friendship with an easy mind. But life, she thought, was seldom as pat as that, and she found it difficult to analyse her feelings towards the tall, broad-shouldered man ahead carrying the child with such ease.

She found it even more difficult to analyse them that evening when he drove her to Ellarton Station to catch her train back to London.

"It's been a good Christmas. Hope you've enjoyed being back with the old gang, Kate," he said as they swung out of the gate of Greenhurst after the last wave from the family at the door.

"Of course I have. You know how fond of you all I am. And I took to your Jean. I'm so sorry for her. I don't think I've ever been so conscious of inner grief, although she hid it so bravely."

"Yes. She's going through a bad time. I think being with us has helped her get through the first Christmas alone. Keep in touch with us, Kate. Don't disappear again."

"No, I won't. I promise."

There was only a scattering of people on the platform and they had a few minutes to wait. In the dark shadow behind a closed kiosk, Mark dropped her case and took her in his arms.

"Someone's kindly hung a piece of mistletoe from that roof, and I don't see why Philippe should have had all the Christmas fun."

It was true. From a pipe protruding from the roof of the kiosk a bunch of mistletoe was dimly discernible, its pale berries caught in the light of a crescent moon. Over his shoulder, the sky was like black velvet pricked with myriads of stars glittering in the frosty air, then his head blotted out the sky. His lips were kind, unhurried. When the train came rattling in he released her and led her to a carriage.

As she leaned out of the window, he said, "Telephone us when you get back. Mother has an odd notion that unescorted young women are at risk these days, but I doubt whether any harm will come to you with these companions."

39

"Goodbye. And thank you, Mark. Thank you for everything," she added as the train moved out.

Her companions consisted of a Salvation Army captain in one corner, reading a journal, two elderly ladies talking earnestly together and one young couple engrossed in each other and prone to giggles. Relaxing, Kate's thoughts were a confused jumble as the train rumbled on. Recollections of Philippe's dark, handsome face, the blood-quickening urgency of his kisses, the desolate pain of Jean Brynton, the dominant presence of Mark, Madeleine's vindictive expression, all jostled in her mind.

Back in her flat, which seemed more bleak and solitary than ever, she telephoned her safe arrival, then unpacked her case carefully, for she had placed Valerie's picture of dried flowers in its midst. It emerged intact, and there and then she set about finding a suitable place on the wall to hang it, for it brought a touch of warmth, a reminder of the way this return to the circle of the Vermont family had brought her into life again after the blankness of the past two years. She was involved again, and in spite of her sister's efforts at indoctrination, that was how she liked to be.

5
A Business Proposition

On a bleak Sunday morning in February, with a sleety rain lashing the windows of her flat, Kate lingered over breakfast in a dreamy mood, reliving the dinner and dance she had enjoyed with Philippe the previous evening, aware of a slight headache, which she attributed to an unaccustomed consumption of wine in Philippe's company, so that she winced a little when the telephone shrilled out. It was Valerie, words tumbling from her in excitement.

"Kate, you did say that you were not keen on your job and were fed up with urban life, didn't you?"

"More or less, yes."

"I'm out of work, as you know, and now a wonderful opportunity has cropped up to run a craft shop in Sussex. For the past few weeks I've been helping out part-time in this shop because the owner had an accident. Now she wants to sell the business. Mark's looked into it and he and Dad are willing to buy the property and finance the business, but Mark stipulates that I have a partner and suggested that you might be interested. Oh Kate, would you? It would be super. We could share the flat over the shop, and it has great potential. We could make it a real craft shop instead of the rather tatty outfit it is now."

"Whereabouts in Sussex is it?" asked Kate, somewhat bewildered by this torrent of words.

"Dilford. Only a few miles from Deanswood, where the Horticultural Station is. Kate, do say it's a proposition that might appeal to you, and come down and hear more about it. I can't tell you all about it on the phone, but Mark's

A Slender Thread

coming home next weekend for a council of war, and we can go into it in detail. I'm so excited at the prospect. You will come, won't you?"

"Yes, I'd like to. I'll . . . "

But Valerie interrupted her with exclamations of delight.

"Bless you! I said you would but Mark thought you might not want to tear yourself away from Philippe. We heard from Madeleine last week that you and he are inseparable."

"An exaggeration. Anyway, Dilford isn't so remote. There's a train service from London, I believe."

"Yes, it's handy enough for London if you're that keen. Are you, Kate? I worry a bit about that possibility. Phil's great fun, but a bit of a womaniser, you know. Anyway, not my business, I suppose. I'd hate you to get hurt, though."

"No risk. Next Saturday, then. I'll catch the ten-thirty from Victoria to Ellarton."

"Angel! I can't wait to tell you all about it. I'll meet the train and you must stay the night. Mother insists."

* * *

Valerie, never a good driver, handled the old family car more erratically than ever that morning as they left Ellarton Station and rattled along the narrow twisting lanes to Cheryton village, words tumbling from her in a non-stop flow until Kate said firmly, "Stop! If we're to reach your house intact, you must leave the intoxicating details of the shop and concentrate on your driving, Val. Wait until you get home and can tell me about it in a systematic way. As it is, I haven't the foggiest idea of what's involved and am risking life and limb at the moment. Look out!"

Valerie braked hard and they nearly slid into the hedge to avoid a car coming round a bend on the crown of the road.

"Too fast," snapped Valerie, "and hogging the lane. All right. I see what you mean," she added with a wry smile.

Winter had still not relinquished its icy grip. The sky was leaden, the hedgerows bare save for a few bedraggled strands of travellers' joy, puddles half frozen. But beneath the holly tree by the front gate of Greenhurst, clusters of snowdrops pierced the gloom with their fragile beauty.

Valerie, almost dancing with impatience while her mother insisted on having a leisurely cup of coffee with them in front of the sitting-room fire before leaving them alone, was at last able to launch forth on an exposition, called to chronological order by Kate.

"I first learned of it from Mark, and he heard about it from Jean Brynton. She knows the owner, and often bought bits and pieces from the shop. It's called The Craft Shop and sells paintings from local artists, pottery, souvenirs of all sorts. You know, the kind of gift shop aimed at tourists. Some good stuff, a lot of tat. I did know it, because I sold a couple of my flower pictures there a few months ago."

"Are there many tourists passing through Dilford, then?"

"M'm. There are one or two well-known gardens and one stately home open to the public in the neighbourhood, and Dilford is a handy place for lunch or tea. It's a pretty little market town in its own right, too. When the owner of the shop had a fall soon after Christmas and was at her wits' end to know how to cope with the shop, Jean mentioned it to Mark. My job had just folded up and he asked me if I'd care to help out. I was glad of something to do. I used Mark's house as a billet during the week and came home for Sunday and Monday, when the shop closed."

"And you liked it?"

"I could see the possibilities. A show case for Sussex craftsmen. An outlet for my flower pictures and for the work of one or two of my art school friends who are having a struggle. I tried to get Miss Redcar interested in that direction, but she said she was too old to start new lines. Since the fall, her health has suffered, and although she's active again now, she decided to sell the business with the flat above, and retire to Wales, where her sister lives."

"And that's where your eyes lit up?"

"Yes. I thought it would be an exciting thing to do, but I've no money to finance such a venture nor any sales experience apart from what I've had these past few weeks. Then Mark had a look over it and discussed it with Dad, and they've offered to set me up if I can find a practical partner. Mark doesn't think I'm very practical," she added.

"But you do know a lot about arts and crafts. I can see its appeal."

"If you would come in with me, Kate, I think we could make a go of it. Mark thinks so, too. He has a high opinion of your competence."

"I'm flattered."

"Apart from your disposition to indulge in romantic fantasies sometimes," said Valerie wickedly.

"I might have known there would be a sting in the tail."

"What do you think, Kate? We could share the flat. It's quite spacious, with a large room under the roof which will make me a fine studio. I've all sorts of ideas bubbling in my head. I'm sure we'd make a good team."

"I like the sound of it. I could put a stake in it, too. When Pamela and I sold our house, which was all we inherited, we had a few thousand over to share between us after the mortgage had been settled. I've hardly dipped into it. We'd need a car to visit any likely craftsmen and collect goods. I can see to that side and do the driving," she added, her experience as a passenger with Valerie as driver fresh in her mind.

Forbidden by her father to use the car during his lifetime, Kate had learned to drive after his death during the months she had nursed her mother. Although she had not wanted a car in London, she had kept her driving licence up to date and, without being an enthusiastic motorist, knew herself to be a safer proposition than Valerie, who now clapped her hands together, her face radiant, as she said, "Eureka! What a lovely, exciting prospect! I can't wait to tell Mark and get down to the nitty gritty."

Mark arrived just before lunch and greeted Kate with a brotherly kiss as Valerie bubbled over with the news that Kate was in favour of the new venture.

"Good," he said. "But since you've no doubt painted a rosy picture of a little shrine of arts and crafts, I'd better go into the practical feasibility of it before she commits herself."

"Always the realist," said Kate, her eyes dancing, for she

A Business Proposition

was in truth half intoxicated herself with the prospect before her, not least because it would allow her to escape from an urban environment which she had discovered was completely alien to her, and savour once more the seasons of the countryside.

"Someone has to keep their feet on the ground."

And that afternoon, Mark, his father, Valerie and Kate went into all aspects of the business, after which Mark pushed aside the papers and figures he had worked out and said, "Are you two quite sure you want to embark on it now that I've made the financial aspects quite clear?"

Nothing but enthusiasm being expressed, he gathered up the papers and said, "Right. I'll instruct my solicitor to proceed on these lines, then."

"Dad, can I sort out your drawings and get some of them framed? I'm sure they'd sell well. Much too good to be hidden away in the attic," said Valerie.

"Of course, my dear. Take whatever you like."

"I'll do it straight away. And I've another idea. The aunts do beautiful embroidery. I wonder if I could persuade them to let us have some of their work."

"I hope you intend to pay some of your suppliers," said Mark. "Leave Val to her dreams in the attic and come for a walk on the heath with me, Kate. I need to work off that steamed golden pudding of Mother's, and Crusoe could do with some exercise. He's getting too fat."

"In this icy weather? It looks like snow," said Kate.

"You've gone soft in London. Come on. A few more things I'd like to discuss with you. We're not going to get any sense out of Val until she floats down to earth again."

They strode out across the heath with Crusoe plunging about through the dead bracken like an animated hearthrug, and were rewarded with a pale gleam of sunshine breaking through the dull grey sky and lighting up some hazel catkins along the path.

"You'll have to be the one who manages this business, Kate. Val's hopelessly impractical, as you know. On the artistic side, she'll be invaluable. The rest will be up to you. I think you can make a good job of it."

A Slender Thread

"I'll do my best. How long do you think it will take to get through all the formalities?"

"Miss Redcar's anxious to be rid of the business. I should think you'd get possession in a month or so if we prod the solicitors."

"I'll give in my notice next week, then. I'm on a monthly basis."

"I hope it will prove a happy venture for you both. I think it will be. I'll be at hand if you need any advice on the financial side. Val's prospects for getting a job to use her talents weren't very bright. I'm glad this cropped up."

"Mr. Fix-it has done it again," said Kate, and although she spoke lightly, the sense of being managed once more niggled at her.

"Pure chance. I'd never have known about it if Jean hadn't happened to mention it. And that reminds me of a favour I want to ask, Kate. Jean moved from the Horticultural Station to a cottage only two miles from Dilford, as you know. I wonder if you'd go and see her sometimes. She took a fancy to you, felt you had much in common, and she's been going through such an awful time, I think it would be a help if you would befriend her."

"Of course I will. I felt very much on her wavelength, too, and desperately sorry for her. I felt her pain like a squeezing hand at Christmas. Is she getting over it?"

"Not really. She's a very sensitive, vulnerable person, and Darrel was her whole life. She looks so fragile, and detached somehow. Even with Diana, she's kind and gentle, but remote, as though she's living in some distant land, lost."

"Has she no other friends?"

"Oh yes, but she shuns them for fear of them talking about Darrel, which she says sets her off weeping again, although I've never seen her quite break down in that way. And she feels she embarrasses them, too. Sympathy is no good to her. She says she'll fight her way through and seek her old friends again one day, but not now. She'd neglected them, anyway, through being so wrapped up in Darrel and the Station. But you're a new face, knowing nothing of her past. I think you could help a lot, Kate."

A Business Proposition

"I'll try. You care a lot about Jean, don't you?"

He was silent for a few moments and stooped to disentangle a length of bramble from Crusoe's shaggy hindquarters before saying, "When I saw Darrel at the hospital that last evening before he died, he asked me to help Jean through the first year. He knew he had no chance. He was very weak, in pain, but his mind was quite clear and his thoughts all for Jean. He told me how vulnerable she was, how closely her life was knitted in with his. We'd all become close friends that last year after Wicklow left and I took over as Darrel's assistant. He thought I could help Jean more than anybody. I should have done my best, anyway, but I was glad to give him a promise that eased his mind a little."

"He left you with plenty to cope with, then."

"Yes. His early death was a huge loss to the Station. It was more or less his creation, you know. He was appointed Director right at the beginning when they moved to Fenton Grange from the old place in Surrey. Fortunately for me, he left it in good shape with a first class team."

"A tough assignment, though," said Kate thoughtfully, for she had noticed a big change in him since they had parted, all boyishness now vanished from his face, which was leaner and gave the impression of being stripped for action, so that he looked a lot older than his thirty years.

"A challenge. It has kept my mind well occupied, anyway, which was no bad thing in the circumstances," he observed drily.

They walked on in silence. It was growing dark, and the sun had disappeared behind the leaden grey cloud cover, leaving the faintest red thread in the western sky. Ahead, the lights of Cheryton village gleamed cheerfully out on the wintry heath. It was Mark who broke the silence some minutes later.

"And how is Philippe?"

"Sparkling, as ever."

"How's the television work going?"

"Very well. They've just finished the first six episodes due to start on the screen the week after next, so look out for the first episode. If the series is successful, and they're very confident it will be, they'll carry on with it. A family saga."

"M'm. Madeleine was telling me about it when she last came down here. Phil is the dashing youngest son of the house, I gather. Sounds tailor-made for him. Unless he's the world's worst actor, he can't be anything but a hit in a romantic family soap opera."

"He has talent as well as great charm," said Kate coolly, a little nettled by Mark's amused tone.

"You'll be basking in his reflected glory, then, as well as Madeleine. Take care there, Kate. Madeleine is very possessive where Philippe's concerned, and more than a little jealous of you, I fancy."

"If that's so, there's nothing I can do about it. She can't expect to keep her brother on a leading rein. Philippe's not the person to be tied down by anybody."

"She's very useful to him, you know."

"Of course. And he appreciates her, I'm sure," said Kate lightly, determined that if he could avoid a direct answer to her about his feelings for Jean, she could be equally evasive about Philippe. It crossed her mind just then to wonder whether Mark had engineered this move from London to put a safer distance between her and Philippe, then dismissed the idea as absurd. His sister was without a job, this opportunity had fortuitously turned up and she was as excited as Val about the prospect. Why was she always imagining that Mark was still managing her as he had done in the past? His life had taken a different direction, and he had obviously accepted that their break was final and indeed sensible, leaving an old friendship which, after all, entitled him to offer advice. It was foolish and irrational always to be on the defensive with him.

But as they neared Greenhurst again, she could imagine Pamela's reaction to this news. "Getting embroiled with the Vermont family again! You're mad, Kate. But Mark Vermont always had you in his pocket."

6
Airborne

" 'Some Enchanted Evening'," sang Philippe softly, his cheek pressed to Kate's as they waltzed around the small square of dance floor in the middle of the hotel dining-room. Kate, happy and relaxed in his arms, wished they could dance on for ever, perhaps on a less crowded floor than this.

"Enjoying yourself?" he asked, drawing her even closer.

"In bliss. That champagne has made me feel airborne."

"And I thought it was me!"

"I'll compromise and say it's a heady mixture."

"Fair enough. I'm not sure that food and dancing should be mixed, though," said Philippe, whose French blood was uppermost in his attitude to food, so that he viewed a dinner-dance as somewhat sacrilegious and almost an insult to the chef.

"If you will start off with oysters!"

"On my birthday, any extravagance is justified. Twenty-six today. And sniffing real success at last, my Kate," he said as they went back to their table.

"I'm so glad for you, Phil. If all the reviews are as good as the two I read, you're in for a long stint."

"I hope so. One or two critics were a bit sniffy, but even so, they thought the public would fall for it, and that's what matters. I need a long stint. Living in London's expensive. And when do you move to Sussex on your new venture?"

"At the end of next week."

"To us, then," he said, filling her glass again.

"Shall I be losing you now to your hosts of admirers?"

"Lose my Kate? Certainly not. I shall expect you to reserve every Sunday for me. Will you be opening this craft shop on Mondays?"

"Probably not."

"Then you'll be able to come to London on Sunday and stay the night with us as often as you like."

"That might not suit Madeleine."

"Madeleine will do as she's told," he said lightly.

"Why not come down to Dilford sometimes? At the speed at which you travel in that sporty car of yours, you should do the journey in well under two hours."

"So I will. You can try to convert me to the charms of the countryside, which I must admit have never appealed since my days on the family farm, and I will continue to initiate you into the joys of London which you seem to have missed before I came on the scene again."

"I loved the holidays in Normandy. Counted the days to them."

"Or to me?"

"Vanity?"

"Of course. Confess now. Wasn't I the main attraction?"

"What girl in her teens could have resisted the lively, handsome young Philippe Touraine? You were everything that was lacking in my life. And we hit it off from the very first day that we met."

"M'm. You cheered up the holidays no end."

But, she thought, if he had known how she felt about him; he had made no effort to keep in touch during the long intervals between holidays, when a letter would have meant so much.

"Play-time. Good times," she said now, remembering the laughter and the zest he had brought to those holidays.

"Then you found consolation with my English cousin. It didn't work?"

"Not quite. We're good friends."

"A bit prosaic, perhaps?"

"Perhaps," she said, reluctant to discuss it.

"I think you were wise. Don't want to take life too

seriously. Enjoy it. If you once get bogged down in marital duties, family responsibilities, mortgages and what-not, it's goodbye to enjoying life."

"You sound just like my sister," said Kate, smiling at him over her glass of champagne.

"The chic and self-possessed Pamela," said Philippe, who had met her at Kate's flat the previous week. "A cool one, that. On the surface, anyway."

"Even you couldn't melt her, Phil. She dislikes all men and sees them as the timeless oppressors of women."

"I shan't waste any time on her, then. I don't like serious women. When you smile, Kate, your eyes crinkle up and you look so adorable that I have to take you in my arms, so we must dance again. It will be a few minutes, I think, before the waiter brings our main course. You see, I put you before food now."

And, his dark eyes sparkling and teasing her, he led her back to the dance floor.

* * *

Kate had postponed telling her sister of her new venture, not relishing the cold water which she would inevitably pour on the scheme. Philippe's arrival at the flat a few minutes after Pamela the previous week to take her to a theatre had helped to delay the disclosure yet further, but with only ten days to go to her departure, there could be no further delay when Pamela met her for lunch the day after Philippe's birthday celebration. The reason behind this summons to lunch was given crisply by Pamela as soon as they had settled at their table.

"I tried to get you on the phone yesterday evening, but no reply. Hope it wasn't inconvenient phoning you at the office this morning. Could you do me a favour and spend next Saturday morning at my flat? The central heating boiler has gone wrong and the people who service it are coming at ten in the morning as a special favour because that was the only time I could be on the spot, and now John has to be in his constituency for the coming week and we shan't be back until next Tuesday. I can leave a note for you to give them.''

''I dare say I can understand if you tell me what's wrong.''

Pamela looked up quickly at Kate's dry tone, then decided to ignore it.

''Thanks a lot.''

They both ordered prawn salads for their lunch and Kate refused a glass of the house wine. While they waited, she said casually,

''I've some news for you. A new job and a move to the country.''

The effect was all that could be desired, for Pamela put down her glass of wine in astonishment. Her astonishment became a cold disapproval as Kate enlightened her further.

''It sounds a crazy scheme to me. Neither you nor Valerie can claim any experience of retailing, and an arty-crafty shop in a country backwater will never provide two people with any kind of a living. I give you six months at the outside.''

''Thanks,'' said Kate laconically.

''You never have been any good at looking after your own interests, Kate. I've done my best for you, and could have done more if you'd listened to me. Just because Valerie Vermont is out of work, you allow Mark - oh yes, I can see he's engineered all this - to rope you in to an enterprise that will never be profitable, just to provide his sister with an occupation and keep you in his sights, perhaps.''

''I've told you. Mark's interests lie elsewhere now. Not with me. That isn't to say we don't remain friends.''

''Then he's using that friendship to find cheap labour to help his sister run a shop.''

''Why have you got this hostile fixation about Mark? You've never had much to do with each other. You don't really know him.''

''I know the type. Male chauvinist to the last breath. I detest his arrogance and his managing ways.''

''Do you know,'' said Kate with a twinkle that robbed her words of ill nature, ''you have just described yourself. This salad is delicious. You certainly know where to find the best meals in London."

"Which you won't find in Dilford."

"I'll survive."

"And what about that handsome Romeo, Philippe Touraine? Aren't you going to miss him?"

"We'll be in touch. Don't tell me that you actually approve of a male," said Kate, teasing, anxious to keep the discussion on a lighter plane, away from the thorny subject of Mark.

"He's a charmer and quite harmless. He'll never have ideas about chaining a woman to domesticity, I guess. I'm not against enjoying yourself with a man, Kate, if you can find a pleasing one. Make use of males for your enjoyment by all means, as they do us. Just don't get trapped into marriage with someone who wants a housekeeper, that's all. You've seen for yourself what that means. Think of the hell of our parents' marriage. Of poor, soft-hearted mother and what that bully did to her, and to us."

"All marriages are not like that."

"Too many. At best, it's captivity for the woman."

"You know, I wonder you don't approve of my venture into a business of my own. Independence and freedom there, surely, instead of being an employee."

Pamela considered this as she sipped her wine.

"I'd be happier if it weren't tied up with the Vermonts. It's messy, combining business with friendship. Doesn't work."

"Well, come down and patronise us when we're established there, and you might get a pleasant surprise. We're full of ideas."

"Souvenir shops for tourists are not really my scene."

"It's not going to be that kind of a shop at all. Real craftsmanship and artistry are what we intend to provide. Things for discriminating people to treasure."

"In a little market town?"

"The country isn't peopled by primitive peasants, you know," said Kate, stung by her sister's contempt.

"Well, I've discovered long since that it's no use

attempting to give you advice. Try not to let your small capital dribble away into the sands of this enterprise, but if you do, I can always find you a job through John's influence." She picked up the menu. "Now, they do a very good crème brûlée here."

But Kate chose a sorbet and turned the conversation to Pamela's political involvement in her employer's constituency, for she had had enough of her strictures. Like their father, Pamela had a way of killing all enthusiasm with a cold sarcasm, and of making her feel inept and hare-brained. While Pamela talked, Kate studied her with a detachment she had seldom before achieved, and came to the conclusion that she was looking at a flawless example of organisation rather than a human being. Perfect grooming, not a hair out of place, her discreetly made-up face framed by a smooth black swathe, was emphasised by the excellent cut of her navy blue suit and white silk blouse. An incisive way of speaking and absolute self-possession made her seem an impregnable stranger. That strong feelings had once lain under that cool exterior, Kate knew only too well from their childhood days, but of late years they had either been frozen out of existence or controlled out of sight. Hitching her wagon to a rising star in affairs of state, her busy life seemed to preclude any emotional element. She never disclosed a great deal about her business life, and as far as Kate could gather, all her energies were engaged in promoting the political advancement of her employer, as well as keeping an eye on the family business of which he was a nominal but not active director.

And while Kate sipped her coffee and listened, she realised with sudden insight and relief that she had come clear of the influence her sister had exerted over her from early days and was now going her own way. The last years of deep distress in the appalling circumstances of her parents' home and the long drawn out, painful death of her mother, had left her drained of all feeling but a need to escape from the old environment and an engagement that lacked romance and raised doubts in the face of her mother's dying pleas to her not to marry, doubts that in her distressed and exhausted state she was quite unable to resolve. In yielding to Pamela's organisation of a new life for her, she had been seeking a breathing space, an escape. It had turned out to be a kind of limbo, but it had given her that breathing space. Now she felt that she had found her feet and was setting out on a new enterprise that presented an appealing challenge in a rural environment to which her heart belonged, for an urban life had proved quite alien to her.

"Well, I must be going," said Pamela. "We've a meeting at three o'clock and I've some papers to sort out."

She signalled the waiter, used a credit card to pay the bill, opened her brief-case and handed Kate a typed letter for the gas service man and a key to her flat. Glancing at her watch again, she added, "I'll leave you to finish your coffee. Thanks for seeing to the boiler for me."

Lifting her hand in a farewell gesture, she walked quickly across the dining-room, a woman of purpose. We go on our different ways now, thought Kate, and dismissing Pamela from her mind, dwelt on her own way ahead with optimism. The prospect was sunnier than any she had looked on for many a year. An exciting job, old friendships renewed, and, burnishing all, a blossoming romance with the enchanter of her teens whose spell was no less potent now in her twenties.

The attention of a man sitting at a neighbouring table was caught by her dreamy expression and the fugitive little smile hovering on her lips. Nice, glossy brown hair framing her face and leaving her broad forehead clear. He was tired of young females peering out from long fringes like sealyham terriers. A creamy skin. Tender, generous mouth. He could not see her eyes, bent on her coffee, only long dark lashes. Not a beauty, but definitely appealing. An innocence there, too. That was a refreshing change. He wondered what she was thinking of, and if he could catch her eye. Then pulled himself up sourly. Verging on middle age, developing a paunch. What foolish nonsense was this? Sentimental conjectures about a girl with a Mona Lisa smile. He'd better recall his mind to the problems awaiting him at the office.

And collecting his bill, he departed in a somewhat dyspeptic mood.

*   *   *

A tedious session in Pamela's flat off Victoria Street, with the gas boiler not being restored to order until late that morning, had Kate scurrying to keep an appointment with Philippe at a restaurant near his flat in Kensington, after which he had proposed a visit to the Tate Gallery to see an exhibition of French Impressionist paintings. He was waiting for her outside the restaurant and brushed aside with a smile her apologies for being late.

"I've had a better idea, Kate, after seeing the menu here. Not very tempting. Let's collect some cold food from a delicatessen I know and have a meal at my place. Never fear," he added, seeing her expression, "we shall be on our own. Madeleine has gone home to the farm for a couple of weeks. She caught an early plane this morning. My mother hasn't been too well, and Madeleine thought it time to see how they're getting on. She's been pining a little lately for Normandy, and, as well, she plans to spend a few days in Paris before she comes back."

"You make me feel guilty. It's not that I dislike your sister, Phil, but I'm afraid she doesn't like me."

He laughed and took her arm.

"Madeleine's always been jealous of my girl friends. Take no notice."

In the delicatessen, tucked away in a narrow street behind Philippe's flat, was a mouth-watering display of food worthy of the sumptuous presentations she remembered in the delicatessen windows of Dieppe. They came away laden with bottled mussels, smoked salmon, ham, salad niçoise, French bread, some Brie cheese and a bottle of wine. A bunch of grapes and some pears bought from a nearby fruiterers completed their purchases.

The Touraine flat had large, airy rooms, a pleasant view over a square of grass and trees, and was kept in spotless order by Madeleine and a help who came in two mornings a week, but Kate, who had only been there twice before, never felt at home there. Somehow, it lacked warmth. It was too tidy, too regulated, reflecting Madeleine's personality rather than the happy-go-lucky ways of Philippe. But by the time they had set out the meal on the dining-table, the bright March sunshine had worked round to flood the room, and when Philippe put on a record of piano music to accompany their meal, it became Philippe's room rather than Madeleine's and Kate's spirits rose to match his.

In a rather dizzy state after the wine, she helped him clear the table afterwards. He insisted on dumping the dishes in the kitchen sink.

"Our Mrs. Green comes in on Monday mornings. She'll clear everything up. I like this waltz. It's an old one. Do you know it? 'Charmaine'. From generations back."

To the lilting music, they waltzed round the room. Philippe was a naturally good dancer, and they moved as one.

"I don't want to go and look at pictures, my Kate," he said softly, kissing her cheek as they danced.

"No?"

"I think it would be nicer to go to bed with you."

They danced in silence, Kate feeling dizzy and confused.

"Don't you think that's a good idea?" he said, as the record ended, and he cupped her face between his hands.

Afterwards, she found it hard to explain her reluctance. She was in love with him and he aroused feelings in her that she had never experienced before, but something was wrong. She could not feel fully committed, or perhaps Madeleine's condemning presence was making itself felt there in her flat. And deep inside her there was a faint sense of shock. He ran his hands down her back, moulding her to him, but she released herself and said gently, "No, Phil. Not now. Not here."

"But there will never be a better opportunity, my sweet." He drew a finger down her nose, his dark eyes reproachful. "You are grown up now, you know. Not playing games in the orchard." He had drawn her into his arms again and was kissing her.

"I'm not sure. Don't rush me, Phil."

He released her then, and smiled, but there was a little edge to his voice as he said, "You must take these pleasures on the wing, my dear, not as a result of careful thought. You have the English failing. Sex is fun. Not solemn. But you are still a little girl in the orchard, perhaps."

"I'm sorry. I need time to sort myself out. You've swept me along so fast these past weeks."

"No matter. We'll drive round to the Tate and see the pictures, after all."

If to Kate the atmosphere felt a little strained between them that afternoon, it was no fault of Philippe's, for he was as lively and attentive as ever, but she felt perturbed, unable to concentrate on the pictures in spite of Philippe's enthusiastic guidance.

Over tea, in a little café nearby, he gave her a quizzical look as he said, "It's all right between us, my Kate. Stop worrying. There will be time. I must leave you soon. I've a dinner date tonight with a V.I.P. in the entertainment world, and his wife. Could mean a lot to me. Open doors. So I mustn't be late."

"You're on the way up, Phil. I'm sure of that."

"It's all starting to happen. But I'll need luck, too. It's a tough profession."

"And you love it. What is its appeal? Acting."

"Hard to say. I'm easily bored with everyday life. Acting different roles, you can project yourself into different lives. Change. Variety. The monotony of that dreary life on the farm drove me nearly crazy. I hate dull routine."

"One crowded hour of glorious life
    Is worth an age without a name,"
she quoted with a smile.

"True, my Kate. But there will be many crowded hours, I hope. Sorry we can't spend the evening together, but I'll be in touch to winkle you out of your Sussex retreat."

He drove her to her flat and kissed her affectionately before they parted.

"Good luck with your V.I.P." she said, and watched him drive off until the little red car vanished round the corner.

Dear Philippe, she thought. He was never angry, never sulked, and had a knack of making her feel dizzy and airborne, as though floating high above the ground, now soaring, now dipping, now hovering, now swooping, like the gliders she had once watched from an escarpment in Shropshire.

But now, she had to come down to earth and start packing up for her move to Sussex.

7
The Night of the Party

By the time Kate joined Valerie, they had had possession of the premises for two weeks, during which time the shop and flat above had been re-decorated, so that they were able to plunge straight away into the task of stocking the shop, organising the little room behind the shop into an office, and furnishing and settling into their flat. Valerie had already done much towards discovering craftsmen anxious for a shop window for their work, and assembling stock, but to her intense annoyance and dismay, she fell victim to an influenza virus a week after Kate joined her and was forced to go home and be nursed, leaving Kate to carry on. She was away for a week, which covered the Easter weekend, and croaked her apologies to Kate over the telephone on Good Friday.

"I feel so mad, leaving you in the lurch like this, but my legs still won't support me, and Mother insists on keeping me here for a few more days. She says she would have liked you to come for Easter, but won't let you take the risk of catching the bug. Dad is the latest victim."

"So sorry. My love to you all, and don't worry about this end. I'm up to my eyes, and loving it."

"But it will be a bit miserable, Easter all on your own."

"There won't be a dull moment, I assure you. I'm getting the office organised, about to buy a car from the owner of that bookshop opposite the war memorial, who aims for better things in the car line, and then I plan to varnish the display shelves. No time for Easter this year."

The Night of the Party

And so it turned out. If Kate felt a little disappointed at not hearing from Philippe over the Easter weekend, she was too busy to fret about it, although conscious of a little niggling fear that their last meeting might have cooled his feelings towards her.

Valerie bounced back after Easter to fling herself into the final preparations for their opening, and on the Thursday evening before this momentous event, Mark turned up to do some odd jobs where male strength and reach were called for. Since his practical approach and Valerie's artistic foibles were often at odds, Kate viewed with some amusement Mark's growing exasperation and Valerie's procrastinations.

"If you'd made up your mind where exactly you wanted to have these pictures hung, Valerie, it would have saved me a lot of time," said Mark after changing the position for a black and white drawing of Dilford High Street four times.

"It's a question of getting the best light for it. Isn't it a lovely drawing? Such fine detail," she said, examining the picture with pleasure. "Real talent, this young man. I'm sure we'll be able to sell his work readily."

When Mark had completed the tasks allotted to him, he downed tools and said, "I propose to take you two to the Royal Swan for a meal. I bet you haven't had a square meal for days, and if you're not famished, I am."

Mark's proposal meeting with immediate approval, they were about to leave when the telephone rang. It was Philippe, asking for Kate. His voice came to her, eager and with that note of laughter in it which was so familiar and dear.

"I'm giving a little dinner party here on Saturday, a rather special one, dear Kate. My V.I.P. and his wife are coming, and I specially want you to meet them. You must come."

"I'd love to, Phil, but we're hectically busy here. We open the shop on Tuesday, and there's still a lot to do."

"Just one evening, chérie. You can stay the night with Pamela and get back to the shop on Sunday morning, if you must. I phoned Pamela this evening to see if she could give you a bed. Unfortunately, our spare bedroom is stripped down for decorators. Pamela said she has a couch which turns into a bed."

"Yes, I know."

"I invited her to join us, out of politeness, you understand, but she's already committed. I can collect a spare key from her first thing tomorrow morning. So you see, I have it all nicely arranged, and you simply must give me this opportunity to show off my girl to my friends."

Put like that, she could not refuse, nor did she wish to, happy at this confirmation that her niggling fears were groundless. Her face was radiant as she joined the others, patiently waiting by the door, and Valerie reassured her about going.

"Do you good to get away for some fun for a change. You've been working flat out ever since you got here, while I was away a whole week, being cosseted in bed."

They elected to walk the short distance to the Royal Swan on the outskirts of the town. It was a fine, mild night, with a full moon rising, and Kate flexed her shoulders, glad to stretch her limbs after spending most of that afternoon crawling on the floor cutting out curtains for the flat. The High Street, with its old-fashioned bow window shop-fronts, petered out at the war memorial square, and the Royal Swan marked its end, a half-timbered inn opposite a bridge across the river. Valerie suggested a short walk along the tow path before they had their meal.

"I need to get the smell of paint and varnish out of my system," she said, "and it looks inviting in the moonlight."

Mark went into the inn to reserve a table before joining them on the path beside the gently flowing river, a silver ribbon between bushy banks. Kate's thoughts dwelt on Philippe, delighted at his desire to make public their commitment to each other and the prospect of the party. She scarcely heard Valerie and Mark discussing the craft shop until Mark said with an incisive edge to his voice that broke through her thoughts, "If you'll remove your romantic hat for a few minutes, Kate, and adopt a practical one, we might have your attention."

"Sorry," she said coolly. "What was it you were saying?"

"That your ideas on book-keeping seem a bit hazy, and you'd better have a session with the accountant I recommended, to start you off. Inspectors of Taxes have a nasty way of wanting proper accounts," he concluded drily.

How typical of Mark, thought Kate, nettled, to want to talk about book-keeping on a spring night bathed in moonlight which rippled on the water and brushed the blackthorn bushes with ethereal beauty. There were pale clusters of primroses here and there on the opposite bank of the river, faint traces of their fragrance on the air. No romance in Mark. But on such a night, she had no wish to remove her romantic hat, and beyond agreeing to make an appointment with the accountant, she retired into her thoughts, wishing it was Philippe walking beside her to savour with her the beauty of that April night.

At the end of that evening, Mark gave her a very curt good-night, scarcely able to conceal his exasperation with her dreamy mood, but Kate, standing at the shop entrance with Valerie to see him off, watched the tail light of his car disappear with her mind already on the party ahead.

* * *

A babel of voices came from the sitting-room of the flat when Kate arrived, but Philippe, who opened the door to her, drew her through the little hall into his bedroom so that they had a few minutes alone together. He kissed her and then held her at arm's length with an approving smile.

"New coat?"

"Yes. My last spending spree before I left London."

"Emerald green. Just right with your colouring. When I'm rich, I'll buy you an emerald necklace, my Kate."

He took her coat and overnight case, and again signified his approval when he saw the maize-coloured silk jersey dress which she had bought at the same time.

"You've done me proud. There will be some envious eyes on me this evening. Now come and meet my friends."

A Slender Thread

Part of Philippe's charm for her was his way of giving her confidence, of making her feel attractive, after years of criticism from her father and more tellingly from Pamela had undermined her, so that when he led her straight away to Paul Winburg, the impresario, and introduced her with evident pride, she greeted this important person with a happy, confident smile, quite at ease. Winburg was a stout man of about fifty, with dark hair peppered with a little grey, shrewd blue eyes, and a formidable jaw.

He greeted Kate with a pleasant smile and said, "So this is the treasure Phil's told us about, while keeping you well hidden."

"Who wouldn't, with all this competition lurking," said Philippe, waving his hand to the rest of the party before turning to the woman at Winburg's side and introducing her.

"This is Paul's wife, Caroline, Kate. The sternest critic of my television performance."

"Not true. Critic of the part written for you. Not of your acting. You do all that's possible to make it less of a cardboard cut-out. But don't let us bore Kate by talking shop before she's had time to get her bearings. I'm so happy at this chance to meet you, Kate. I've heard so much about you from Philippe. You're just starting up a craft shop, I hear. You must tell me about it later on," said Caroline with a dazzling smile.

She was a slim woman of average height, with dark hair pulled smoothly back from a pale oval face, regular features and fine dark eyes. Dressed in a black velvet suit with a diamond brooch and matching drop ear-rings, she had a low, pleasing voice and a warm manner. Very attractive, thought Kate, and some years younger than her husband.

If her reception was warm and friendly from the rest of Philippe's friends, consisting of three couples and two unattached men, it was in contrast extremely cool from Madeleine, who addressed her with the polite formality of a stranger, but Kate, with Philippe always in close and fond attendance, felt happiness bubbling inside her like a fountain that evening, untouched by his sister's reserve. But

The Night of the Party

if Madeleine lacked warmth as a hostess, she produced an excellent dinner, displaying French cuisine at its best, and with wine flowing freely, it was a sparkling party. Much of the banter and talk was of show business, which Kate found interesting if a little out of her sphere, but she finished up having learned a lot about television from a producer who entertained her with hilarious accounts of awkward moments and near disasters behind the scenes, which had, it seemed, in no way diminished his cheerful confidence. With Philippe on the other side of her, she enjoyed herself immensely, and, glancing round the room when she was momentarily alone later that evening, she decided that Philippe's world was both charming and exhilarating, and that its gaiety was infectious.

But not, apparently, where Madeleine was concerned, for Philippe's sister was talking to Paul Winburg with the serious, disapproving air of a headmistress lecturing an unsatisfactory pupil. How odd that she could so closely resemble Philippe in looks and yet so utterly lack his lively charm. She was wearing a burgundy coloured dress, simple and well cut, adorned only with a silver, star-shaped brooch on the shoulder. As Kate admired the French chic which Madeleine conveyed, the latter looked across the room at her as she talked, and Paul Winburg followed her eyes, so that Kate felt sure that they were talking about her. A little discomfited, she turned with relief to Philippe, who came up and put an arm round her shoulders and kissed her cheek.

"Enjoying yourself?"

"Immensely. A lovely party."

"And my girl, the star. All lit up and sparkly." And there and then in no way inhibited by the presence of his friends, he cupped her face between his hands and kissed her lips lingeringly, smiling afterwards at a few appreciative whistles and jocular observations. She was still blushing when Philippe slipped away to replenish some glasses and Paul Winburg joined her.

"I'm not going to let young Phil monopolise you. This room's very warm. I need to cool off, and perhaps you do, too," he said, smiling. "Come and sit by the window and tell me where you met our rising young star."

Happy and confident, Kate willingly told him. He listened to her account of the holidays in Normandy with flattering interest.

"Well, that's really romantic. Refreshing in this hard-boiled age, that sort of constancy. And it all went on from there?"

"There was a gap of a few years when circumstances were against our seeing each other, but it was always there, and when Phil came over here to live, it was . . . well, just as it always was, only better."

"Progressing a little too fast for his sister, perhaps," he said with a quirky little smile.

Not knowing quite how to respond to this, Kate nodded ruefully. He patted her hand.

"Not to worry. Madeleine is a little, shall we say, puritan? Not in tune with our English scene. Things are a little less free and easy in French middle-class families, I believe, and although Madeleine is only half French, she was brought up in France."

A little confused by his words, but remembering that this man was important to Philippe, she merely smiled and said, "She can be a little prickly."

"That, I think, is an understatement. But Phil can protect you, I'm sure. Fate was just a little unkind . . . weekend . . . a . . ."

His last words were drowned by an outburst of laughter nearby until it subsided enough for her to hear him again as he patted her hand, saying,

"Phil's a lucky young man. He's got a bright future in front of him. That means rival claims, though. Show business is a bit hard on lovers. You going to be able to let him go when his career makes demands? I've seen too many couples come to grief, because being in love makes one possessive."

He was jumping ahead, she thought, but Philippe's attitude that evening could have left nobody in doubt of the nature of his commitment to her. More than a little dizzy,

The Night of the Party

she was spared having to reply to Winburg's little homily by the arrival of his wife, who swept Kate away with an eager barrage of questions about the craft shop.

The Winburgs were the last of the guests to depart just after midnight, and Caroline asked Kate if they could give her a lift. "Or perhaps you're staying here," she added.

"No. I'm staying the night at my sister's flat."

"And I'm driving her there," said Philippe, coming up behind Kate holding her coat.

"Taking no chances of upsetting your good sister this time," said Paul Winburg softly and with a little chuckle. "Hard luck, but I think you're wise." He raised his voice as Madeleine joined them from the bedroom carrying Caroline's fur jacket, and said, "See you and Madeleine at my office on Wednesday, then, Phil. We'll settle the details of the contract then. Think no more of that letter. With the success you're having, you're bound to make a few enemies. Ours is a bitchy business."

And with warm thanks to Madeleine for her hospitality, they took their leave. Sitting beside Philippe in his car as they drove round to Pamela's flat, Kate said, "What was all that about? Upsetting Madeleine and making enemies."

"Oh, Madeleine didn't like one or two clauses in a contract I'm signing with Paul for making television films. She's my agent, you know, and a jolly hard-headed one, too."

"Making enemies?"

"Oh, that's nothing," he said, half laughing. "Someone trying to put a spoke into my wheel. You were a great success tonight, you know. I was proud of you. You really enjoyed it, didn't you?"

"Yes. Couldn't fail to with that lively lot. I feel a bit sleepy now, though. It must be the wine."

He kissed her goodnight on the doorstep of Pamela's flat with an affectionate hug.

"You're a grand trooper, Kate. Be in touch soon."

She crept in quietly to find the couch in the sitting-room made up into a bed for her and a cryptic note from Pamela lying on the pillow.

A Slender Thread

"Don't disturb me before nine tomorrow morning. I'm flaked out."

Restless in the unfamiliar bed, Kate's thoughts flickered over the party, her head still in a whirl over Philippe's ardent attentions in the presence of his friends. Always lively and affectionate with her, this evening had been different. Less flippant, more deliberate. As though making it quite plain that they were in love, now and for all time, to an extent that at times had faintly embarrassed her. But then Philippe had no inhibitions. Feelings were for displaying, which was why he was a good actor.

She could not make up her mind whether she liked Paul Winburg or not. He had made her feel a little uneasy, she could not say why. And she was sure he and Madeleine had been discussing her. Had he been vetting her, to see if she would make a suitable wife for his new-found star? She doubted whether Madeleine would have given her a good reference, for her hostility was barely concealed. Dismissing these pinpricks, which barely counted in her enjoyment of the evening, she fell asleep at last with Philippe's dark, handsome face and his warm kisses her last thought.

8
Mishaps

Leaving the busy main road with some relief and driving along a narrow, twisting lane, Kate was able to reflect that a sunny May morning in the English countryside was hard to beat. She was on her way to the Vermont aunts, Grace and Lucy, to collect some needlework they had done for the shop. They lived in a Surrey village about an hour's drive away, and this was an expedition she had gladly undertaken, for she remembered them with affection in the days of her engagement to Mark and had since never failed to send cards on their birthdays and at Christmas.

The lane was margined with the white flowers of wild parsley, giving it a bridal look, and yellow celandines gleamed brightly on the banks. The first white blossom was out among the fresh green leaves of the hawthorns, and daffodils and tulips brightened front gardens. She drove round the cricket green, past the squat little church with the mossy porch, and down a narrow side lane to a small russet brick, tile-hung cottage bearing the name 'Cobblers'.

The aunts greeted her warmly, produced coffee and homemade oatmeal biscuits in the tiny garden behind the cottage and plied her eagerly with questions about the shop.

"The first week was quiet, and we were feeling our way, but we've been busy this week and it looks promising."

"Such a lovely idea," said Grace, "selling the work of craftsmen rather than machines. A joint venture for you and Valerie. I'm sure you'll make a success of it."

"Depends if there are enough discriminating people

A Slender Thread

around," said Lucy, "but if Mark thinks it's viable, it probably will be. He's got a good practical head on his shoulders."

"And how is dear Mark?" asked Grace gently. "We haven't seen him since Christmas."

As they chatted on, Kate eyed them with affectionate admiration for the way in which they kept old age at bay with a youthful zest and interest in life which made it difficult to believe that Grace was seventy-three, and Lucy two years her junior. They must have been pretty girls, thought Kate, and wondered why they had not married. Grace, small, rosy-cheeked, with pale blue eyes and white hair, had a gentle manner and a childlike sense of fun which cloaked a shrewdness that had often surprised Kate in the past. Lucy, more sturdily built, with fluffy grey hair and fine dark eyes like Mark's had a more down-to-earth manner than her sister, and to those who did not know them well would appear to be the dominant partner, but the Vermont family knew that it was the gentle little Aunt Grace who led, equipped as she was, Mark said, with sly weapons disguised as posies, used with a subtle skill which delighted him.

The sun was warm on Kate's face as she leaned back in her deck-chair and let the serenity of the little garden wash over her. Always, it seemed to her, the aunts had created at 'Cobblers' a charmed retreat from the world, tranquil, well ordered, as she imagined a convent might be. They had never grown out of the Edwardian era of their childhood, and although they took a lively interest in individuals and in every member of all branches of the Vermont family tree, they took none in the troubled affairs of the world at large, and lived out their lives, devoted to each other, independent, and always happily occupied.

The garden was full of the fragrance of wallflowers and humming with bees busy among the tulips on this, the first really warm day of the summer. The latest news and state of health of all members of the Vermont family having been touched on, the outstanding progress of Evelyn's boy, Jeremy, remarked upon, they came inevitably to the success of Philippe.

"We've never seen a great deal of the French connection," said Lucy. "It really is most exciting to have Philippe and his sister living in England now."

"And I believe we're going to see them both at your luncheon party on Sunday," said Grace. "We're so looking forward to it. What a lot to celebrate! Your flat-warming, shop-warming, Valerie's twenty-fourth birthday, and Philippe's success on television. We haven't a television set, you know. We really prefer the wireless. But we have a good friend nearby who invited us in to see the first episode of the serial Philippe stars in. Most interesting. And Philippe was splendid. So handsome and dashing. I couldn't see much of his mother in him. He must take after his French father."

They chatted on as though she were a member of the family, made no allusion to the breaking off of her engagement to Mark, and if they knew of her involvement with Philippe, as she was sure they did, for they were always up to date with all family news, they ignored it.

A blackbird was enjoying a vigorous splash in the bird-bath nearby, scattering glistening drops of water over the forget-me-nots below. At the mention of Philippe's name, Kate's heart warmed at the prospect of seeing him again, showing him the shop and the flat. She had neither seen nor heard from him during the two weeks since that heady night of the party when he had claimed her so openly, for all to see. It was Madeleine who had accepted the invitation on their behalf when Kate had telephoned them, Philippe being absent.

When she aroused herself reluctantly to go, for she had some pottery to collect on her way back, the aunts brought her their work, a tapestry fire-screen displaying a bunch of cottage garden flowers worked in glowing colours by Lucy, and two white silk blouses exquisitely made and embroidered by Grace. Kate congratulated them, marvelling at the skill which old age had in no way diminished.

"You all have so much talent with your hands, you, and Valerie, and your brother."

"Roland is the most gifted. Some of his drawings and

A Slender Thread

paintings would have made him famous, I'm sure, if he'd had any gift for promoting himself, which he hasn't. I always thought it a pity that he became a commercial artist," said Grace, convinced that her young brother was an undiscovered genius.

"He had to earn a living for his family. Anyway, Roland's always enjoyed his work in his own way. Not ambitious," said Lucy, "and all the better for that, I'm sure."

The artistic talent which Roland Vermont shared with his sisters and had bequeathed to his youngest child, had not surfaced in either of his other two children, thought Kate, for Mark and Evelyn had both inherited their mother's competent, practical nature, although Mark's liking for and considerable knowledge of music had its roots perhaps in the artistic sensibilities of his father's side of the family.

They stood at the front gate under the lilac tree, with its fragrant white blossoms reflecting the sun, to wave her off, little rosy-cheeked Grace in her pale blue cotton dress topped by Lucy's smiling face with its halo of grey hair.

"Until Sunday," called Lucy, "and a grand celebration."

But it did not turn out like that at all.

*   *   *

The weather, in its fickle way, had turned grey and chilly on the Sunday morning, but Valerie's skilful window dressing made the bow-fronted shop look warm and inviting, they had filled odd corners of the flat with tulips and irises for a festive look, and had spread a sumptuous buffet feast in the large living-room, all of which more than made up for the cheerless aspect outside. They would number thirteen in all, but as Valerie was superstitious, she counted Jeremy, who had just passed his sixth birthday, as only a half. Adding the final touches to the buffet with two bowls of fresh fruit salad, a large oval dish of smoked salmon slices encircled with wedges of lemon and a large fruit flan, they were interrupted by the telephone.

Mishaps

"That was Mother. Dad fell off a ladder in the garden yesterday evening. He was sawing a broken branch off the apple tree, and has twisted his knee and bruised sundry parts. They'll be coming with the aunts, who are spending the weekend with them, but won't be staying long after lunch, if we don't mind, because Dad is a bit shaky."

"A good thing your mother can drive the car. Don't look so worried. I'm sure she wouldn't let your father come if it was at all serious."

"True. We'll bolster him up with champagne."

Barely ten minutes had elapsed before the next damper was applied in the shape of a telephone call from Madeleine which Kate took.

"Philippe is terribly sorry, but he won't be able to come to the party today. He's away on location in Yorkshire shooting a film for television and expected to get back last night, but things haven't gone quite right, and they'll be up there for a few more days."

"I'm so sorry," said Kate, her spirits plummeting. "How are you getting here, then, Madeleine? I presume Phil has the car."

"Yes. There's a train to Dilford at eleven-five. I shall catch that. It arrives at twenty past twelve and if your shop isn't far from the station, I should arrive in good time."

"It's only about ten minutes' walk. Turn right outside the station and the shop is half way along the High Street on the left hand side. If I'd known earlier, I could have arranged for Pamela to pick you up."

"It will be an easy journey for me, thank you. With Philippe away so much, I shall really have to get a little car of my own. Now I must go."

Cool and businesslike as always, Madeleine hung up, and Kate gave the news to Valerie.

"A pity. Phil is always such an asset at a party. And it meant a lot to you – his coming. That's what comes of being attached to a famous man. I hope it won't spoil the party for you."

"Of course not. Your birthday. Our flat-warming. The launching party for this remarkable partnership," said

73

A Slender Thread

Kate, linking her arm in Valerie's and hiding her disappointment with a smile. "It's going to be a splendid occasion, whoever turns up. No doubt about that."

But in spite of their efforts, that luncheon party did seem to lack a little sparkle, with Valerie's father trying to hide the fact that most movements were painful, the aunts fluttering round him a little anxiously, and Madeleine giving an impression to Kate of a smouldering tension. Congratulations on the attractive appearance of the shop window and approval of the flat were universal, however, and Mark, who had arrived with a bottle of wine under each arm and a package for his sister containing a thin silver chain with a finely wrought pendant, helped things along, teasing the aunts, who adored him, and warm in his praise of the achievements of the new partnership.

They browsed round the shop after the first welcoming drinks. The plain pale grey walls showed off well the drawings and etchings of Roland Vermont, some watercolours of local scenes from an artist who lived in a village a few miles from Dilford, and Valerie's flower pictures. On one side of the shop they displayed pottery, glass paperweights, baskets and hide leather purses and shoulder bags, all the work of craftsmen in the county. On the other side were hand-knitted sweaters, lace clothes and the silk blouses grouped round Aunt Lucy's fire-screen. They had been agreeably surprised by the number of craftsmen in the county who were glad of a shop window for their work, and with odd spaces in the window filled with items of porcelain which Kate had found at a country house sale and obtained for a modest price, they were well stocked.

"This is lovely," said Pamela, fingering one of the silk blouses. "Am I allowed to buy it out of shop hours?"

"Of course," said Valerie, wishing that they had put a higher price on it for Pamela, whom she had never liked.

Roland Vermont was studying one of the water-colours, and Kate put a hand on his arm gently.

"All right? Really all right?"

He patted her hand and smiled.

"Good enough to enjoy all this. You girls have done well.

Nice brush work, that." He peered more closely at the picture of the path through a wood, shadowy, autumnal. "I'll buy this for Grace's birthday next month. She'll like it," he said, glancing across the shop to confirm that his sisters were having an animated conversation with Evelyn over the hand-knitted sweaters and were out of earshot.

"You don't *have* to buy up the goods," said Valerie, coming up behind them and giving her father a smile. "You weren't invited for that, you know. Just for the pleasure of seeing you here. I wish you wouldn't go sawing branches off trees. You should have waited until Mark was home to do it."

"Your mother's words exactly. In future I shall heed them."

"You know you never do. You've been standing long enough. Kate and I will help you upstairs and sit you in an armchair and bring whatever you fancy from our table of goodies, plus a glass of your favourite white wine which Mark kindly brought with him."

"An excellent programme, dear. Just smuggle that watercolour out to the boot of the car some time without Grace spotting it. I'll send you a cheque."

And supported by Kate and Valerie, he made his painful way up to the flat and an armchair.

The good food and wine induced a relaxed and pleasant mood, but soon after it was cleared away, Marjorie Vermont, noting her husband's tired face, rose and said briskly, "Now, my dears, we must leave you. It's been a lovely celebration, Val. We're very proud of all you and Kate have done."

"Won't you just stay and sample the birthday cake the aunts brought and have a cup of tea?"

"No, darling. We'll leave you young people to enjoy that."

And when Marjorie Vermont spoke in that tone of voice, everybody knew there was no more to be said.

After they had gone, Kate went out to the kitchen to get tea, for they all seemed a little inert after the effects of the wine had worn off, apart from Hugh, who had drunk only

A Slender Thread

apple juice, and was teaching Jeremy to play Scrabble. The little boy, who had been on his best behaviour, was looking sleepy, for he had somehow managed to avoid his father's careful supervision of the food he had chosen for lunch, Hugh having been enlisted by Mark to aid in pouring the wine, so that Jeremy had loaded a plate with veal and ham pie and potato crisps instead of the health-giving egg salad and wholemeal bread and butter which his father would have allotted to him. By creeping in between the aunts while his father was engaged in a serious conversation with his father-in-law on the best way to saw off a broken bough without damage to self, the rest of the tree and the plants growing nearby, Jeremy had also managed to secure a large slice of fruit flan afterwards and had induced Aunt Lucy to pour a generous amount of cream upon it, all of which would have horrified his father, to whom fat in any form was a menace to health. Not surprisingly, therefore, Jeremy's involvement with Scrabble was torpid, to say the least.

Following Kate into the small kitchen, Mark propped himself against a built-in cupboard and watched her as she collected cups and saucers on a three-tiered trolley. His scrutiny was discomfiting.

"Not quite in top form today," he observed. "Disappointed at Philippe's absence?"

Thinking that she had hidden her disappointment very well, she reflected with some irritation on Mark's skill at reading her state of mind. She answered coolly.

"Of course. Phil is always an asset at a party. Would you mind moving? I want to get at that cupboard."

He shifted and said calmly, "Are you and Val hitting it off as business partners and flat-mates?"

"That's a foolish question. Val and I have always got on splendidly, as you know full well."

"Living and working together all day can impose strains on the closest of friendships."

"Not on this one."

"I'm glad. I thought it would work out, but just wondered whether you would find the pull between London and Sussex a bit of a strain."

Mishaps

"Not at all. Would you mind? I want to get a knife out of that drawer."

"H'm. You seem a bit edgy to me. That's a very fine cake, I must say."

Kate, glad of the change of subject, surveyed the cake with pleasure. It was a large fruit cake, iced and decorated with crystallised rose petals and violets round the perimeter and 'For Valerie' traced in elegant script in pink icing across the centre.

"How clever the aunts are! Everything they do with their hands is beautiful, whether it's embroidery or decorating a cake. And I'm sure the inside will live up to its exterior. Aunt Lucy is a splendid cook."

And just then, Hugh put his head round the door with an apologetic air.

"We're just going, Kate. Sorry we can't stop for tea, but Jeremy feels sick. Evelyn thinks if we bundle him into the car and give him a brisk walk across the common at the end of the High Street, we may stave off trouble." He eyed the cake gravely and Kate could not resist saying with an innocent air, "Can I tempt you to a slice now before you go?"

"Valerie must cut it with due ceremony, and Jeremy's condition calls for a swift remedy. Our thanks and congratulations, Kate. We wish the shop every success," he concluded with a rare smile that transformed his thin face.

"Well," said Kate after he had gone, "I'd better wheel this in quickly before the few remaining guests vanish."

"Dear old Hugh!" said Mark, smiling. "I'm willing to bet that young Jeremy will turn out to be a gourmet and wine connoisseur when he grows up after the austerity his father inflicts on him. Still, Jeremy has proved his father's point today. He was looking very green."

"It's a pity Hugh doesn't carry round a bag of muesli with him," said Kate a little tartly, for Mark was right. She did feel edgy.

The party now reduced to five was oddly constrained. Madeleine had never been an easy mixer, and Pamela had

A Slender Thread

never liked the Vermont family. She had only been invited because Kate wished to show her sister the shop to confound the pessimistic opinion Pamela had expressed when first told of the venture. She had seemed favourably impressed, and sat now, sipping her tea, detached, chic in her light grey suit, polite in her exchanges with them, but lacking any warmth. Now and again her eyes rested on Mark, leaning back in an armchair opposite her, his eyes hooded, wearing what Kate termed his poker face.

It was Valerie, attempting to inject some life into the proceedings and fill the silent spaces, who set it off with a harmless remark to Madeleine.

"Did you enjoy your spring holiday in Normandy, Madeleine?"

"Very much, thank you."

"Did you find Aunt Hester and Uncle Henri well?"

"Yes. Mother suffers a little from arthritis, but otherwise they keep well."

Valerie tried again.

"And you spent the last few days in Paris, I heard. How exciting!"

"Yes. I shall be going back again next weekend, to attend the wedding of an old friend."

"Is Phil going with you?" asked Kate.

Madeleine turned to her, eyes blazing.

"No. But don't think you can take up residence in my flat while I'm away, as you did before."

There was a stunned silence for a few moments. Then Kate, staring at her in astonishment, said, "I've never stayed at the flat, Madeleine. What do you mean?"

"What do I mean? You know very well what I mean."

"I don't."

"Then I'll spell it out. I returned home from Paris a day earlier than expected because I'd caught a cold and wasn't feeling at all well. I managed to get a seat on an early plane on Easter Monday, if you want your memory refreshed as to dates. As my taxi turned into our street, I saw Philippe helping you into his car and driving off. It was nine-thirty in the morning. I'd not been able to get Phil on the telephone to tell him I would be coming home a day early. He's seldom in."

"It must have been a friend paying him an early call," said Kate calmly.

Her calmness seemed to anger Madeleine still further.

"In your green coat? The one you wore when you came to our dinner party. I found the remains of a breakfast for two, with nothing cleared away, and all too clear evidence that Philippe had not slept alone the previous night."

"I spent the whole of the Easter weekend here, sorting out the office, varnishing shelves for the shop."

"Really? I doubt whether you can prove that. Will Valerie help you out?" asked Madeleine with a venom that shocked Kate, who said angrily, wishing to spare Valerie embarrassment,

"I was quite alone. Valerie was at her home in bed with flu. But I don't need to prove anything, Madeleine. This is not a criminal court. I've told you the truth."

"You never visited the flat at all while I was away, then?"

"On the day you left for your holiday, we had lunch at the flat before going on to the Tate Gallery to see an exhibition of French Impressionist paintings. Phil left me at tea-time because he had a dinner date with Paul Winburg and his wife," said Kate.

But because memories of that lunch and its aftermath came back vividly, her cheeks flushed and she knew that she sounded less than convincing as Pamela laughed and said teasingly, "Never explain, Kate. It's a golden rule. But if you break it, do it with a better alibi than that."

Mark was studying Kate through narrowed eyes as Madeleine turned a furious face to Pamela and snapped, "I don't consider it a joke."

"I am not called upon to give an account of myself to you, Madeleine," said Kate firmly. "You are not my keeper. Nor Philippe's. But I've told you the truth. I've no more to say."

"But I have. You're lying. You should have taken care to brief Philippe, because he admitted you were with him the night before I arrived home. As he said, who else? You've been trailing him ever since we set foot in England, and if you're so eager and willing, perhaps it's no wonder that Philippe obliged, but I'll not have it going on in my flat as soon as my back is turned. I've made that clear to Philippe, and to you now, I hope."

"Philippe said I was there that night? I can't believe it," said Kate, bewildered.

"He wouldn't lie to me. You . . . '

But here, Mark took over.

"We'll have no more of this, Madeleine. Whatever is between Philippe and Kate is their own private affair. Nothing to do with you. They are both adults, free to live their own lives as they choose. To make accusations in this offensive fashion when you're a guest at a party given by Valerie and Kate is deplorable, to say the least. We'll have no more of it."

"And what's all the fuss about, anyway?" asked Pamela with a look of cool amusement. "We're living in the eighties, not in Victorian times. Women are liberated now. Don't you agree, Mark?"

There was no mistaking the malice behind the little smile that Pamela directed at Mark, whose face gave absolutely nothing away.

"Those may be the moral standards of London," snapped Madeleine, saving Mark the need to reply. "They are not the standards Philippe and I were brought up to in France."

Mark stood up suddenly, putting his cup and saucer down on the table with a rattle that threatened to crack them, and said grimly, "If you want to catch the four-fifty train, Madeleine, you had better get moving. I'll drive you to the station."

"Don't bother."

"It's raining quite hard now, but walk if you prefer."

"Would you like to come back with me?" asked Pamela sweetly. "I can drive you back to London as quickly as the train."

"No, thank you," replied Madeleine vehemently. "I'll accept your offer, Mark, as it's raining."

She uttered only a few frigid words of thanks to Valerie before she went, ignoring Kate, her face as bleak as an east wind in January.

"You'll come back, Mark, won't you?" asked Valerie.

"No, my dear. A good party in spite of the unpleasant ending, but a lingering death is never desirable. Goodbye Pamela, Kate."

He nodded, put a friendly hand on Valerie's shoulder for a moment and followed Madeleine out.

"Well, I suppose I'd better be off, too," said Pamela.

"You didn't exactly help to smooth things over, did you?" observed Valerie indignantly.

Pamela shrugged her elegant shoulders.

"Who could? There's nothing to be done when a neurotic woman loses control."

"You needn't have behaved as though you knew that Kate and Phillipe were lovers."

"No? Aren't they? Their business, of course. I must admit that I found it rather amusing and quaint to see puritanism rampaging in this day and age. Now, where did I put that blouse?" concluded Pamela with a slightly derisive little smile.

Kate, now as pale as the tissue paper in which the blouse was wrapped, but fully in command of herself, slid the package into a carrier bag and handed it to her sister, saying, "I can always rely on your good nature, Pamela, to curdle things, but no matter. I'll see you to your car."

Walking out to the car, Pamela said coldly, "I didn't start it. An absurd fuss about a little fun and games. Not my style, exactly, but then I've never lost my head over any male and don't intend to. You're a fool if you let any man mess up your life. Stick to your business."

"I don't need your advice," said Kate wearily. "I've had enough of that all my life. Just keep it to yourself in future, please."

"Dear me! We are all out of sorts. Personally, I found the last half hour not lacking in a certain piquant humour. I'm not sure that our male chauvinist saw it quite like that, though. I can't deny that it pleases me to see his pride dented, as it must have been, although he gave no sign."

"What do you mean?"

"Why, the thought that his cousin had succeeded so quickly and easily in getting from you what he had failed to win from you in years couldn't be very sweet, could it?"

"You hate Mark, don't you?"

"Hate? I wouldn't bother myself that much over Mark Vermont. But yes, I dislike him enough to enjoy seeing him put down."

"You grow more ill-natured with the years."

"Really? I think you're confusing ill nature with common sense, and an instinct for self-preservation. You were always lacking in that, my dear. So long."

And with an airy wave of her hand, Pamela pulled her car door shut and drove off.

Kate walked slowly upstairs to the flat and found Valerie surveying three plates with half-eaten pieces of cake on them. She looked near to tears and Kate put an arm round her shoulders.

"I'm terribly sorry, Val. I feel it was all my fault."

"You're not to blame for my crazy cousin. Or your detestable sister, needling you and Madeleine and Mark like that. Real spite, if ever I saw it, from both Madeleine and Pamela. I wanted to bang their heads together," said Valerie, who was never less than whole-hearted in her likes and dislikes.

"Why does Pamela hate Mark, I wonder. They've never had much to do with each other, after all."

"Evelyn once said that Pamela found him attractive. Oh, years ago, when you and Mark were engaged. She thinks she angled for him and was rejected with some vigour. She overheard a quarrel between them once. Might explain her vindictiveness. Her attitude to you. Her campaign to alienate you from Mark."

"She never did that. I was always fond of him and still am."

"I know. Well, it's all old hat now, but she showed her claws all right today."

"It was to have been such a happy day, and somehow it

Mishaps

all went wrong. A spoilt party for your birthday, Val. I'm so sorry."

"No need to feel sorry for me. You were the victim."

"It was horrible. I can't understand it. Madeleine saying I was there at Easter. Perhaps she was making that up to confirm her own suspicions, but she sounded so certain. And then saying that Philippe confirmed it. I don't believe that for a moment."

"Well, it's none of Madeleine's business, anyway. It's crazy, her possessiveness where Phil's concerned. Crazy and unnatural. Let's not talk about it any more. I reckon we'll be eating that birthday cake until next Christmas."

They set about clearing up and said no more about Madeleine's outburst, but Kate was determined to see Philippe at the earliest possible moment and clear things up.

Worrying about it in bed that night, her mind went back to the party where Philippe had made so much of her. She remembered Paul Winburg's sly innuendoes, his references to Madeleine's puritanical streak, some remark about a weekend which she hadn't quite heard, and seeing Madeleine talking to him across the room and feeling that they were discussing her. Unhappy at the humiliation she had suffered at Madeleine's hands that evening, the amusement Pamela had derived from it and the utter impassivity of Mark's face, it was a long time before she could get to sleep, although she told herself that Philippe would clear it all up when she saw him.

9
End of a Dream

"It was awful, Phil. In front of Pamela, Valerie and Mark. Ruined the tea-party."

"Oh, you shouldn't pay any attention to Madeleine. She's always been jealous of my girl friends. You know that."

They were walking in St. James's Park on that sunny Sunday morning, with the trees showing the first fresh green leaves, and brilliant red tulips blooming in the flower-bed they were passing, but Kate, for once, had no eyes for the beauty of spring.

"I couldn't help paying attention. Nor could the others. It was a really venomous attack. Didn't she say anything about it to you?"

"No. But then I haven't seen much of her, since I only got back two days ago. Forget it, love. I'll have a word with her."

"But she made a definite accusation which was untrue, Phil. And she said you'd admitted that I spent the night with you on Easter Sunday."

"Wish you had. Too good a morning to discuss my sister's lectures. Put it out of your mind, Kate. Better things to think of."

He had his arm through hers and pulled her closer, smiling at her. They walked in silence for a few moments, then Kate said quietly, "Just tell me the truth, Phil. That's all I want. Looking back, I think that Madeleine told Paul Winburg that you and I were having an affair, because at that party he was all nudges and winks, so to speak. I took no notice at the time, but I realise now what it was all about. Madeleine saw someone leaving your flat with you early on Easter Monday morning. She thought it was me. You said it was me, but it wasn't. So, just tell me what's really been going on. I'd like to know."

He gave her a sidelong glance, and then, to her astonishment, his eyes sparkled with mischief and he chuckled.

"All right. It's really rather funny, and you mustn't be cross, my Kate. I don't think you will be, because you're my dearest friend and would always be game to help me out of a scrape, I'm sure."

"Go on."

"In confidence, of course."

"Of course."

"Well, it was Caroline Winburg who stayed the night. Paul was on the Continent. Caroline brought a script round for me to have a look at, and . . . well, business turned to pleasure. Unluckily for me, someone sent an anonymous letter to Paul saying he would do well to enquire about the whereabouts of his wife that weekend. Did he know that she and a certain new young star, initials only given, were so intimate? You know the sort of thing."

"I don't, but go on."

"Well, you understand that I can't afford to get on the wrong side of Paul. He was a bit grim when he showed me that letter. I denied it, and said my affections were engaged elsewhere, with you."

"And that I was with you on the night in question."

"Yes. I knew you wouldn't mind getting me out of a fix."

"But I wasn't asked, was I?"

"Look, love. I was in a nasty fix. Paul had phoned Caroline that night from the Continent, and she was missing. He is a very important man in the show-biz world and can do a lot for me, and wants to. But not if I'm having an affair with his wife."

"That seems reasonable," said Kate in a tone as dry as desert sand.

"I had to convince him that the letter was the work of someone who had it in for me. Success doesn't make you popular with everyone. Not in our profession." He glanced at her uneasily, and Kate took the story on.

"And so you put on that act at the party, aided by Madeleine, but you deceived her, too, because she really thought it was me."

"I didn't have to tell her. She knew it was you before the words were out of my mouth. After all, it was the natural thing to assume, and Caroline did have a coat very similar to yours which my sister spotted as she left. When I told her about the letter Paul had received, she was horrified. She knows what his influence means to me."

"And so she made it clear to Paul at the party that I was the favoured one on the night in question, and you made it clear for all to see. That explains Paul Winburg's attitude to me that night and his remarks to you as he and his wife left about the letter and making enemies, which you explained away airily when I asked what it was all about."

"Well, that was neither the time nor the place for lengthy explanations. It worked. Thanks to you."

"It worked because you manipulated us, Madeleine and me. You took our feelings and used them for your own ends. We were just characters in a bedroom farce which you'd scripted. I would never have thought you capable of doing that in a thousand years, Phil."

"Come, Kate. Don't turn it into a melodrama. You're taking it all too seriously."

"I'm afraid I can't see anything funny in Madeleine accusing me at our party of sneaking into your bed the moment her back is turned. I didn't notice the rest of the audience rolling in the aisles, either."

"You *are* angry, aren't you? I agree that it was inexcusable of Madeleine and I shall tell her so, but don't let it spoil our day. I've a special restaurant I want to introduce you to for lunch. Live for the day, my Kate."

She gazed at him in amazement. To him it was no more than a play. She was in love with him. She had thought he was in love with her since the party. But it was all an act that night, put on to deceive Paul Winburg. And he seemed to view his affair with another man's wife, and that man his

End of a Dream

benefactor, as a lark which had threatened to turn awkward for him, and Kate herself as a handy scapegoat. She remembered Valerie saying that when they were children, Philippe always slid out of trouble and others got the blame. He had not lost any of his old skill, she thought bitterly.

"Do you intend to carry on your affair with Caroline Winburg? Because I'm not going to be your alibi again."

"Heavens, no! Too risky. It just happened. We were in the mood. Nothing serious, Kate. You're a bit old-fashioned, you know. We were just having fun. But it seems that's not much in your line, judging from the way you turned it down when offered."

"Casual sex? No, it's not my line."

"Well, I'm sorry if I've been a bit naughty. Let me make up for it with a good lunch and some champagne. I've just concluded a very nice contract with Paul. We must celebrate."

"I'm afraid you must excuse me, Phil, and find another stand-in. I expect honest dealing from my friends, especially one who was as dear to me as you were. I realise now that the Philippe I was in love with was a myth left over from my teens. Forgive me for being so naïve."

"Don't be silly, Kate. We're old friends. This self-righteous attitude doesn't suit you. Come on, now. I've said I'm sorry for Madeleine's absurd carry-on. Now let's forget it," he concluded, putting an arm round her shoulders and giving her a coaxing smile.

She saw, then, that further words about it would be fruitless. They simply did not see it from the same angle. She blamed herself for having been so blind, and spoke with an effort.

"All right, Phil. No hard feelings. But this is goodbye."

"Nonsense. I don't believe it."

But something in her expression as she looked at him with painful intensity warned him that a wind of change was blowing them apart, and his smile faded as she said drily, "You're on the brink of a very successful career. We shall watch it with interest. I underestimated your acting ability. You'll go far, Phil. Goodbye."

A Slender Thread

And she walked rapidly away. Philippe looked after her, shrugged his shoulders, and carried on walking in the opposite direction.

Sitting on a seat by the lake, oblivious of the people around her, of the ducks, of the children feeding them, Kate's unhappiness turned to anger. She had been used with a callous disregard for her feelings, Philippe's sister had insulted and humiliated her in the presence of her friends, and Philippe saw it as nothing more than a naughty comedy. And her anger turned then on herself. How could she have been so blind to Philippe's true nature? She had been warned by both Valerie and Mark, who had known him from childhood. She had been flattered by his charm and apparent delight in her at that first meeting at Christmas, a delight only caused, she saw now, by her all too obvious admiration and calf love for him. His vanity sucked up admiration as a bee sucked honey. In reality, he loved only himself. His self-protection was of the highest order, his looks and his charm honed to that end. She had adored him when she was an impressionable young girl, and had carried his picture in her heart ever since, like any stage-struck child. And had in fact never known the real Philippe Touraine, only the Prince Charming of her imagination.

In calmer mood as she walked through the park to the Mall and headed for Victoria Station, reflecting unhappily on this destruction of all her illusions, she realised that to Philippe, lies were not lies but merely another form of acting, and that integrity did not enter into his calculations. There could be little doubt that his affair with Caroline had consisted of more than one impulsive night, to give rise to an anonymous letter to Caroline's husband. He would go through life, she thought, skimming off its pleasures, enjoying his success, escaping from the boredom which so easily assailed him by acting many different parts, perhaps hurting many hearts in the process, but too much of an egoist even to notice it. It would be foolish to grieve for the loss of such a man, but the pain of the destruction of a long cherished dream was real indeed and it would be a long time before she would forget that last hour of their party,

End of a Dream

Pamela's amusement and Mark's grim impassiveness. The damage caused then would live on, she feared.

Unable to face any food, she snatched a cup of coffee at the station before catching a train back to Dilford. Valerie had gone home that weekend and so there was nobody in the flat to see her white face and the tears which she could not restrain once she was alone.

*   *   *

Sensitive as always to her friend's feelings, Valerie's face expressed concern when she saw Kate on her return to the flat on Monday evening but their exchanges were brief.

"Were you able to sort things out with Phil?"

"Yes. It's finished between us, Val. I've been foolish. Should have heeded your warning. Let's not talk about it."

"He only ever was a party man, Kate. A professional entertainer. I knew he would hurt you."

Kate managed to meet Valerie's troubled eyes with a little smile.

"It's all experience. I suppose, in a way, I asked for it. A silly romantic, as Mark would say."

"Don't blame yourself. Phil could charm the bark off a tree."

"Only a very immature tree," said Kate with a little gleam of humour which cheered her friend. "Now tell me what's going on at Greenhurst. Are they well?"

"In good form, except for Crusoe who got a nasty bite from an unfriendly bull terrier and is immensely sorry for himself. He shouldn't be such a friendly old noodle. Perhaps it will teach him to be more cautious."

"Crusoe and I are in the same boat, then."

"You could say that," said Valerie with a little smile, but, looking at the dark shadows under Kate's eyes, she knew that Crusoe's wound would heal the more quickly.

"Well, now to business. I shall be able to concentrate better now," said Kate with a determined air. "I've a couple of calls to make tomorrow. That country house sale at Deanswood, and some dolls' clothes to collect from the aunts."

A Slender Thread

"I've brought a couple of Dad's sketches back in my case. Rather nice. One of the bridge over the river where we walked last Christmas, and another of the village green."

And the subject of Philippe was dropped. Thereafter, however, Valerie was apt to refer to him as the party man.

For Kate, a post-script to the affair came in the form of a letter from Philippe which she received two weeks later.

My Dear Kate,
No after-thoughts, then? I am sorry you took that little escapade so seriously. Just wanted to say that I shall always feel a great affection for that holiday girl of our salad days. I somehow always see you in the orchard at home, helping me pick the apples, the girl with the chestnut hair and grey eyes and lovely smile. But I've moved on since then, Kate. My mistake in expecting you to have moved on, too. Forgive me. And thanks for the memory.
I leave for Italy tomorrow – the location of our next T.V. film.
      Adios,
       Philippe

It was a clever wriggle out of guilt for a dishonest piece of manipulation from a master of that skill, thought Kate with a wry twist of her lips as she tore the letter up and threw it into the wastepaper basket. A grain of truth there, though, to rub into the wound. She had been ingenuous, had carried over a schoolgirl romance and endowed it with qualities that had little foundation in the realities of the present. She had returned to earth with a painful crash, and not the least painful part of it was the prospect of facing Mark, whom she had not seen since that disastrous party. She could not assess the damage there, only remember Pamela's ill disguised taunts.

Unhappy and uneasy, she returned to her task of writing up the books, finding figures easier to deal with just then than human beings.

10
Adrift

Kate's fears about Mark's reaction to that ugly scene with Madeleine were confirmed when he came to the flat one evening at the end of May in response to a call from Valerie for help in putting up some more shelves round the shop. His greeting was brief and businesslike to Kate and tinged with exasperation towards Valerie.

"I'm not a carpenter, Val, and I do have a lot on my hands just now. Get someone in the locality. Anderson's a good chap and will be glad of the work."

"Can't afford it. Anyway, if you'll just give a little advice about what wood to order and the fittings, we can do it ourselves. Don't want strangers trampling round."

"Only your long-suffering brother. I'll take you at your word and act as consultant only," he concluded firmly.

"All right. That's all I wanted."

"Was it?" asked Mark, smiling a little and tweaking Valerie's fair hair.

"Well, of course, I know how good you are at such jobs, and so good-natured, as a rule," replied Valerie sweetly.

"Flattery will not work, my girl. Putting up display shelves isn't such a simple job as you seem to think. It calls for a proper carpenter. It will be a legitimate expense to put against your tax. Get Anderson."

"Tax? We may not make enough to pay any."

"You will. You've not started at all badly."

"I don't know about that."

"Of course you don't. You never have had any head for figures. Perhaps you'll get out the books and let me have a look, Kate."

He spoke as to an employee, and looked at her as though at a stranger. She felt suddenly cold. Never in all the years of their friendship had Mark looked at her like that, with the polite formality of a slight acquaintance. She fetched the books from the office and he glanced through them. While he did so she moved to the window and gazed out as Valerie went into the kitchen to make some coffee. If the atmosphere seemed full of tension to Kate, Mark made no sign of being aware of it. When he had finished his inspection, he said, "As I thought. You've started pretty well."

"Yes. We're quite pleased, really. Mark . . . I must apologise for Pamela and that scene at the party here. I . . ."

"Please, no post mortems," he said, interrupting her. "How you conduct your affairs is no business of mine, and you are not responsible for your sister any more than I'm responsible for Madeleine. It was Val whose party was spoiled, though, which was a pity. There's no more to say."

"But . . ."

"And that's final."

His face was implacable, his voice calm but so decisive that she felt as though he had cut some line between them and left her adrift. She looked at him in dismay, but Valerie came in just then with a tray of coffee and they resumed their discussion of the installing of the shelves in the shop. It ended, as was inevitable, in their agreeing to call in a carpenter. Mark did not linger long, and left with scarcely a glance in Kate's direction.

"Well," said Valerie, "he was a bit east-windish today. But I dare say he has headaches at the Horticultural Station. A lot of responsibility and a large staff to manage. I suppose our shelves might seem a bit trivial."

"We're so used to calling on Mark. Taking him for granted," said Kate.

"I know. He's so capable and usually so helpful. I expect he's right, though. We do need a proper carpenter."

Kate nodded and hid her dismay. Ever since her childhood, she had taken Mark's concern for her as part of the established order of things. Now that it was withdrawn, she felt as though a warm cloak had been taken from her. Even during the two years she had spent in London, she had always felt he was there, in the background, and when she had met him again afterwards, she had felt warmed again by his friendship, as though there had been no interval. Now, without that cloak, she felt cold and unhappy. Unreasonable, perhaps, in all the circumstances. She tried to rally herself. Where was her spirit of independence? The enjoyment of freedom from personal entanglements so strongly recommended by Pamela? She had the shop to involve her. She had Valerie's loyal friendship. But with her love affair with Philippe in ashes and her friendship with Mark obviously over, it still felt cold.

* * *

Assailed by guilt at how little she had done to fulfil the promise made to Mark to befriend Jean, for her absorption in Philippe and her occupation with the shop had filled her time to capacity, she drove to the little cottage one fine June evening bearing an anthology of poetry which she had discovered in a second-hand bookshop in Dilford. It was her own favourite anthology, long out of print, and knowing Jean's love of poetry, she had snapped it up when she saw it.

The cottage was only a short drive away, on the edge of a village consisting of no more than a dozen cottages, an inn and a small Saxon church. It had been a hot day and the evening sun seemed to have cast a golden spell over the little village, for there was no movement to be seen there, and the only living creature in sight was a black cat slumbering by the lych-gate of the church, paws neatly tucked in. As she stepped out of the car, the cat opened wide green eyes, gave her an unblinking stare, rolled over on its side and went to sleep again.

The cottage windows winked back at her as she walked up

A Slender Thread

the flagged path. Half-weather boarded, with red bricks below, its walls adorned by a rampant honeysuckle on one side and a less exuberant clematis on the other, the cottage slumbered in the sunshine. The porch was shaded by a white rambling rose, one strand of which caught at Kate's hair as she pressed the bell at the side of the oak door. It evinced no reply. Guessing Jean to be in the garden, she walked round the side of the cottage and at first could see no sign of her. Then she saw her sitting in the shade of an old apple tree at the far end of the garden, reading. As Kate stood there, Jean put the book down and cupped her eyes, as though they hurt her. She looked a lonely figure, sitting there. When Kate called, she looked up and quickly brushed her hands across her eyes, managing a smile as she came to meet her, although her eyes were bright with unshed tears.

"This is a nice surprise," she said. "Come and join me on the seat. It's cooler out here."

There was no doubting the sincerity of her pleasure at receiving the anthology, and they chatted easily together of poets and writers, of the shop and of Diana.

"It's her fifth birthday in July, so school is looming. I shall miss her. She's a good little companion. But it will be good for her to have more friends."

While Jean went into the cottage to make a pot of tea, Kate picked up the book which Jean had been reading. It was a collection of essays and poems by Mary Webb, and the bookmark opened it at a poem entitled 'The Difference'. She read the first verse and understood why she had found Jean almost in tears.

> I walk among the daisies, as of old;
> But he comes never more by lane or fold.
> The same warm speedwell-field is dark with dew;
> But he's away beyond a deeper blue.
> A year today we saw the same flowers grow –
> Last May! Last May. A century ago.

Solitude and poets were not, perhaps, the best recipe for Jean Brynton at this stage, and Kate determined to become a frequent visitor, for they had much in common and she had taken a warm liking to this gentle, sensitive woman so badly in need of consoling friends.

"I love this time of the day," said Jean as she poured the tea. "So peaceful. And mysterious, somehow. Neither day nor night."

The scent of pinks hung on the air as the garden darkened and a crescent moon rose over a clump of trees on the distant downs. Soon, only the ghostly white flowers of some lilies in the border stood out of the shadows, and the grass became wet with dew.

"Come in and hear a lovely recording of some Schubert impromptus that Mark brought me last week, just to round off the evening."

Left alone for a few minutes in the sitting-room while Jean went up to see that Diana was sleeping peacefully, Kate's eye was caught by two photographs on the bookcase against the wall. One was of Jean's husband. Kate had met him once at an open day at the Horticultural Station when Mark had introduced her, a tall, dark man with a strong face and an assured but pleasing manner. He looked far less formidable in this photograph, taken in the garden, smiling, with Diana perched on his shoulder grasping his hands. The other photograph was of a group of two couples and a third man, Jean and Darrel making up one couple. It must have been taken many years ago, for Jean looked a laughing young girl with Darrel's arm round her waist. Indeed, she was scarcely recognisable, with rounded cheeks and a face full of vitality. The other young couple struck a more serious note; a rather lowering young man and a good-looking girl with dark straight hair hanging smoothly to her shoulders, a rather strained little smile on her lips.

Jean, returning and seeing her interest, said, "That was taken on a winter holiday we had with some friends at Menton in the south of France. It was such a happy holiday that we had the photograph enlarged and framed it as a reminder. That was five years ago, before Diana was born. It seems a lifetime ago now."

Only five years ago, thought Kate. She would have

A Slender Thread

thought it farther back than that, for Jean looked at least ten years older now than that laughing young woman in the photograph.

"Who is the odd man out? The fair Adonis on the other side of you."

"Nick Barbury. A very old and dear friend of ours."

"Nick Barbury, the writer? Biographer."

"Yes."

"To have such looks and talent seems almost unfair."

"And he's as nice as he looks, too. Cool. Witty. And very kind when you know him."

"Do you see him often?"

"No. He married a few years ago and lives in France. He writes now and again, though, and always remembers Diana at Christmas and birthday times. He's her godfather. Now for some music," added Jean. "Clifford Curzon plays these so beautifully."

They sat in the soft light of a single lamp on the bureau as they listened to the music. Kate, by the open window, watched the starry sky, feeling the music steal over her senses, banishing all frets and heartaches, wrapping her in a spell of pure delight. The moon sailed high in the sky now, like a silver feather, and no leaf stirred in the shadowy garden on that still summer night.

Jean thanked her with unmistakeable sincerity when Kate took her leave.

"It's been such a lovely evening," she said.

"And for me. Can I come more often?"

"Please. If you can spare the time."

Kate hesitated, afraid to tread on too sensitive soil, then said gently,

"It is getting better for you, Jean?"

"Yes. It's the little things that let me down now and again. Silly, really. A song, or the way Diana looks sometimes, or even a plant in the garden that Darrel treasured, can overthrow me, and the tears come again. It's embarrassing for my friends. But getting better," she added, with more firmness than accuracy, Kate suspected.

Driving home in thoughtful mood, Kate reflected that

although people talked glibly of getting over things, one never really got over a bereavement of the kind Jean had suffered. You learned to accept it, that was all. They must have loved one another deeply. And she found herself wishing that one day Jean might find a consoling love again, for she seemed such a vulnerable person on her own.

11
Revelations

The sun was beating down fiercely on the little garden at 'Cobblers' and the aunts had moved the chairs into the shade of the cherry tree. On the low wooden table beside them stood a jug of home-made lemonade in which some ice cubes were rapidly melting.

Kate sat down with a sigh of relief and gazed with pleasure at the spectacle of Aunt Grace and Aunt Lucy, who had the gift of never looking or seeming hot or flustered. The heat-wave was now in its third week and showed no signs of waning. Scarlet oriental poppies blazed in the borders and the pots of geraniums on the narrow paved area behind the cottage equalled the poppies in vibrant colour. Close at hand, the soft cool mauve of a cluster of Maggie Mott violas beloved of the aunts was as soothing to the eye as the drink was to her parched throat.

"This is heavenly," she said. "The car was like an oven this morning, and I got caught in a traffic jam near Horsham. My own fault. I should have taken the by-roads."

"Such a lovely summer," said Aunt Grace. "Like the ones we seemed to enjoy so often in our childhood, although memory plays tricks. I'm sure there were plenty of dismal, wet summers, but they're not the ones you remember. And of course there were hardly any cars on the roads then. Not where we lived. The only vehicles I can remember were the milk float and an occasional coal cart."

"We bowled our hoops up the road to the common in perfect safety," said Aunt Lucy.

Revelations

"And whipped our tops in the road. You were very good at that, Lucy. I could never keep my top spinning as long as you could."

"And do you remember how lovely it smelt after the dust-cart had been along sprinkling water?"

"Indeed I do. And the smell of tar when they did the road. That held us spell-bound, watching the bucket of hot tar being swirled over the road, then those flip-flop rubber brushes pushing it round and smoothing it over, then shovels of little stones scattered across it. A fascinating operation. We usually managed to get some tar on our clothes, much to our mother's annoyance. I can't help thinking that life was more fun for children then," concluded Grace.

"I'm sure that riding on top of a tram-car or an open-top bus was much more fun than riding inside a car. Those trams used to buck up and down like ships at sea."

"And the horse brakes when we were on holiday. They were exciting. Do you remember how the horses bolted that time at Clacton? We thought it thrilling, but Mother was scared and lectured the driver afterwards."

"And how dusty the hedges were always. But full of wild flowers."

Kate smiled, intrigued by a mental picture of the aunts whipping tops and bowling hoops along empty roads around their home at Clapham Common. She loved to hear them in a reminiscent mood, conjuring up such a different world, and encouraged them to go on, saying,

"I can picture it all from the drawing that Mark's father did of the road where you lived. He showed it to me one day. Tree-lined, large old Victorian houses, lamp-posts and a lamp-lighter there with his long pole. He drew it from a photograph he'd taken long ago. It was a delightful picture. It all looked so stable and secure, somehow."

"And at the top of our road, just by the common, there stood that lovely little Italian cart with lots of brass taps and the friendly man who sold the sarsaparilla. And the muffin man came round, too, of course. Dear me! How very old we must be!" exclaimed Grace, but her lively blue eyes, smooth pink complexion and quirky smile might have belonged to a young girl.

When, reluctantly, Kate had to leave them, for she had other calls to make, Aunt Lucy fetched the object of her visit, a set of doll's clothes which Kate had commissioned from them for a birthday present for Diana. Inside a tissue-paper lined box was a white silk party dress with a lace trimmed bodice, puffed sleeves and a pink sash falling down the full skirt, together with a little pink quilted cape trimmed with white fur. Beneath this was a second layer consisting of a blue skirt, a red woollen jumper, a blue and red scarf and red hat with a blue pompom on it.

Delighted with these exquisitely made little garments, Kate said, "Well, Pulsatilla will certainly be the best dressed doll in Sussex."

"I hope they fit," said Aunt Grace, fingering the party dress as though reluctant to let it go.

"Jean gave me the measurements, so I'm sure they will. Diana adores that doll. It was sent to her from France by her godfather two years ago, and is her constant companion. I know she'll be delighted with these. Bless you both."

Kate went to Jean's cottage that evening to leave the birthday present with her. Diana's birthday was still a week away, but she was eager to share with Jean her own pleasure in the aunt's work. It was a beautiful evening, cooler now that the sun was sinking, and she decided to walk instead of driving, for she had been shut up in the car for long enough that day. By taking a short cut across the fields, she could walk it in half an hour, and she set out, glad of the exercise and the peace of the countryside.

The footpath across the field wound through the long flowering grasses of high summer among which daisies and scabious were blooming. By the hedge, in the shade cast by two hawthorn trees, some horses were grazing. Across a stile and down to a stream, she stopped to watch two swallows dipping and swooping after insects, their rapid fluttering wings giving them a miraculous turn of speed. Out to the lane, fringed by the white lace of cow-parsley, she walked the short distance to the village, then through the churchyard, where yellow vetch and thyme made a colourful carpet between the old lichen-covered gravestones, and so to the cottage. Outside was Mark's grey Rover car.

Knowing that they would almost certainly be in the garden, she waited only a moment after pressing the doorbell before walking round the side of the cottage, then stood transfixed. At the far end of the garden, Jean and Mark were locked in an embrace that forbade any interruption. Mark was holding Jean's head against his shoulder, murmuring some endearment. Her arms were clasped round his shoulders. It fell on Kate like a blow between the eyes. Stunned at first, she became aware of a violent protest welling up inside her. No, no, her mind seemed to say over and over again. Aghast as much at her own passionate reaction as at the sight of that close embrace which showed no sign of breaking up, she crept back and walked away from the cottage with trembling legs. Sitting on a seat just inside the church gate, she tried to collect herself. Was it so surprising? She could not but be aware of Mark's affection for Jean, his concern for her unhappiness since Darrel had been killed. And what more natural than for Jean to seek comfort from a person as kind and supportive as only Mark could be? She knew that comfort from her own experience of his support through the unhappiest times of her home life, when her father's cruel tongue had driven her sometimes to despair, knowing that she could not desert her mother, his most vulnerable victim.

She had no idea how long she sat there, trying to recover her self-possession and beat down the violent protests of her heart and mind, but when at last she moved, the sun had set and the sky was darkening. A light appeared in the sitting-room window of the cottage as Kate walked up the path. She had decided just to leave the parcel with Jean and not go in, for she still felt unsure of her ability to appear her normal self.

"You must come in for a few minutes, Kate. Mark's here. We've just cooled off enough in the garden to enjoy a pot of tea. Do come and join us," said Jean.

It was difficult to refuse, and Kate followed her into the cottage, rigid with the effort to betray nothing to the man who

A Slender Thread

had always been able to read her face so accurately. Jean's face was flushed, her eyes bright, as she brought Kate into the sitting-room. Mark looked very much at home in the armchair by the window, leafing through a copy of *Country Life*.

"A late call," he observed after she had greeted him with what she hoped was a passable smile. Jean left them to fetch another cup and saucer for Kate.

"Yes. I waited for it to get cooler before I walked here."

"It's been a scorcher. You look a bit knocked up. Too hot for you?"

"I had a lot of driving today, and I was cooked in the car."

She was busying herself unwrapping her parcel, and avoided his gaze. When Jean returned, she was able to show her the doll's clothes and enjoy her obvious delight with them. Resolutely cheerful, Kate chatted about the aunts and their vistas of earlier times, then about the foibles of some of the shop's more eccentric customers, aware all the time of Mark's thoughtful scrutiny. She felt that she was talking too much, but was filled with an almost panic-stricken urge to keep the ball rolling until she could get away. Her two companions contributed little. They were wishing her away, perhaps.

Then, when she had run dry, Mark said, "I've two tickets for the violin and piano recital at the Dilford Arts Centre next Saturday evening, and am trying to persuade Jean to come. She needs a baby-sitter she can trust. Val's going home on Saturday evening for the weekend, so I wondered if you'd mind stepping in, Kate, if you're free after the shop closes. Jean is reluctant to ask such a favour."

"Yes, I'm free and I'll be glad to sit in for you, Jean. A chance to have a quiet read."

"Are you sure? It seems a bit of a cheek to ask you, but I would love to hear the Beethoven Spring Sonata. I remember the violinist at the school of music I attended in my salad days. He's travelled far since then," said Jean.

"Of course you must go. No trouble for me. What time would you like me to come?"

Jean looked at Mark, who said,

"I'll pick you up at six-thirty, Kate. No need to drive over yourself. The concert begins at eight o'clock, and will probably end by ten, so it won't mean a late night."

"Right," said Kate.

"Now, Jean, there are no obstacles, and it will do you good to have an evening out for a change. We can have a meal beforehand at that restaurant next to the library. It's very good, I'm told."

"And leave Kate hungry? No. I'll have a nice little cold meal ready here for the three of us. That will be lovely. Thank you both for being so kind," said Jean.

For Mark now, thought Kate, she was just like an old pair of slippers. Handy to make use of. Perhaps she always was. Romance was never there. He was probably annoyed at being denied a cosy dinner with Jean, but she was not going to refuse Jean's suggestion. His face, however, when she looked at him, did not register annoyance. Was it a gleam of amusement? She was not sure.

She rose to go, the need to escape urgent, and found her legs unwilling to support her, so rigidly had she been holding herself under control. She could not rid herself of the picture of Jean in Mark's arms.

"I'll drive you back, Kate. It's too dark a night for you to walk," said Mark firmly, seeing the hesitation in her face.

And much as she longed for the darkness of the night to hide her, to escape and be alone with her chaotic distress, the car would get her home in ten minutes and she felt unequal to the walk across country in the dark. She had intended returning before darkness fell, but her sojourn in the churchyard and Jean's insistence on her staying for a cup of tea had used up the daylight.

Sitting beside Mark in the car, as she had done so many, many times in years gone by, she felt choked. As he switched on his headlights and they moved down the lane, he said,

"Thank you for coming to the rescue, Kate. Jean's not had an evening out since Darrel's death. She needs to get out in the world again."

"Yes." For the life of her, she could say no more.

A Slender Thread

After a few minutes' silence, he said, "And how is Philippe?"

"I haven't seen him for some weeks. The last time I heard, he was off to Italy to make a television film there."

"So that's why you're fretting. Val said she thought you were not in your usual good spirits, and you look a bit peaky to me."

"I am not fretting for Philippe," she snapped, her nerves suddenly at breaking point.

"He's playing hot and cold, is he? Well, we warned you. But you never did see the real Philippe, did you? Only the romantic hero of your dreams."

Perhaps it was as well that he had now provoked her to anger which for the moment blocked the distress that had threatened tears.

"I don't need you to lecture me on my personal affairs, Mark."

"Maybe not, but I'm going to, because I know my cousin far better than you and I don't like to see you getting hurt because of your foolish illusions about him. You're not the first to be dazzled by his charms, and you certainly won't be the last. There's no future in it, Kate, only unhappiness, because you're just not Phil's sort of girl."

"And what sort of girl is that, may I ask, since you appear to have all the answers."

"A good-time girl, here today and off to another affair tomorrow. Nothing serious."

"Highly desirable, given the character of most men." Was that her voice, she wondered, that sounded like splintering glass?

"Perhaps, but unfortunately yours is not that kind of nature."

"Are you such an expert on my nature?"

"Yes. And I wish you'd get off this silly high horse. I've known you intimately since you were a skinny child in a grey skirt and school blazer, and why you're in such a thundering bad temper just because I mention a few home truths about my cousin, I don't know. Perhaps making me suffer for Phil's sins. Is that it?"

"I've no intention of discussing Philippe with you, Mark. Why are you stopping here?" she added, as he drew up in the entrance to a farm a short distance from Dilford.

"Because I don't like driving while I'm having a row."

"No row as far as I'm concerned. I'm tired and I just want you to drop me at the shop as soon as possible. I don't know why you choose to lecture me now. You've been distant enough during the past weeks to make me think that lectures from you were a thing of the past."

He leaned on the driving wheel, turning to her.

"I was angry with you for getting into such a mess with Phil and courting trouble with Madeleine. For being so starry-eyed and immature. In that mood, I preferred to keep my distance until I could be more objective about it."

"And now you can be."

"Yes," he said calmly.

It was very quiet in the car after he had switched off the engine. Ahead of them the lane was like a black tunnel between the overhanging trees.

"I can walk the rest of the way," said Kate.

He caught her arm as she went to open the door.

"Don't be childish. Let me say this first. I care about your happiness, Kate. As a family, we all do. You know that. In a way we feel responsible, since Phil is our relative and we brought you together. But you've picked a bad lover in that young charmer, my dear. Constancy is just not in his nature. The longer the affair goes on, the more disillusioning and unhappy it will be for you. Cut your losses and break away before the damage spreads further."

"And who says Phil and I are lovers?"

"Madeleine, for one. And she's on the spot, after all."

"And you, for another? Although I denied it."

"You denied that specific occasion. I believed you. But you looked as guilty and confused as any schoolgirl caught out of bounds where earlier opportunities were concerned. On that, I had an open mind."

"Keep it open," said Kate sweetly, "and drive on, please."

Her blood was up now as she wondered just how he would react if she lectured him about making love to Jean.

A Slender Thread

"You've often made my palm itch, Kate. It does now," he said grimly. "You deserve all you'll get from Philippe."

"Well, thank goodness you've stopped being altruistic and lecturing me for my own good."

At that, in the infuriating way he had of disarming her, he laughed and said with genuine amusement in his voice, "You were always a good scrapper, Kate. But not quite as touchy as you are now. Being crossed in love is hard on the nerves, though."

He started the car again then, and sitting there in the dark beside him as they moved forward, she was unable to decide which urge was the stronger, to hit him with a blunt instrument or to feel his arms round her and rest her head on his shoulder, as Jean had done.

Valerie was in the studio working on a notice for the shop window giving opening times. Absorbed, her fair hair gleaming in the light of the table lamp, she looked up only briefly before returning to her task, and Kate was glad not to be the focus of her attention.

"I've finished the price tags. Thought I'd work on this. It's too hot to go to bed. Feels thundery. Think we might have a storm."

"Yes."

"Was Jean pleased with the doll's clothes?"

"Very. Mark was there. He's persuaded Jean to go with him to the recital at the Arts Centre on Saturday. I've promised to baby-sit for her."

Valerie leaned back and surveyed her work, then said, "Do you think there's anything brewing between Jean and Mark?"

"Could be."

"She's four or five years older than he is, and wedded to the memory of her late husband, but that doesn't mean she wouldn't like other consolation. I like her, but I wouldn't be ever so happy to hear that Mark was going to marry her. Of course, I can see they have things in common. Love of music, the Horticultural Station. But I don't think it's exactly ideal, living in the shadow of a previous adored spouse, do you?"

"No. But I can't see Mark taking second place for long in those circumstances."

"Oh, we're probably quite wrong in our guesses. He promised her husband to see her through the first year of bereavement, and Mark keeps his promises very thoroughly. My brother also plays his cards close to his chest. Never gives much away. No use trying to pump him. His response would not be all sweetness and light."

"Too true," said Kate and leaned over Valerie to watch her put the finishing touches to the notice. Being Valerie, it was no plainly printed notice but one of beautifully executed Gothic lettering within a framework of entwined flowers and leaves. "That's lovely, Val. Worth a price tag of its own."

"Dad does this sort of thing better than I do, but it's not bad. Think I'll do a 'Closed' notice now. Our existing one's a bit mundane."

"Well, I'm to bed. Don't work too late."

Although she felt tired, Kate found it impossible to sleep. She heard Valerie come to bed in the room adjacent to hers just before midnight, and shortly after that, she gave up all idea of sleeping and got up, slipping into a thin dressing-gown to sit on the window seat by the open window. There seemed no air, the atmosphere heavy and sultry. Beyond the High Street she could see the dark huddle of woods and a church spire against the sky. As she leaned her head against the wall, she faced the fact that she loved the man she had rejected nearly three years ago, that she had been chasing a romantic will-o'-the-wisp in Philippe, and had discovered the truth too late. She had little doubt that Mark had found love again with Jean and that he retained only a casual, friendly affection for her. And perhaps, she thought, there were no unhappier words than 'too late'.

12
Holiday Plans and Problems

Jean had prepared a tempting meal for them of cold salmon, salad, raspberries and cream, accompanied by a light Moselle wine. Giving this the measured enjoyment it deserved resulted in a hurried departure by Jean and Mark in order to get to the recital in time, and left Kate, like Cinderella, to clear the meal away and wash the dishes in spite of Jean's instructions to her to leave everything in the kitchen sink.

She endeavoured to occupy her mind after these chores had been completed with the calming world of Jane Austen and *Pride and Prejudice*, but with only partial success, her mind straying to Mark and Jean as often as it was concerned with Elizabeth Bennet and Mr. Darcy. Half way through the evening she went upstairs to Diana's bedroom, thinking she had heard a cry, but found the little girl sleeping soundly, her dark hair tousled, one arm stretched across the pillow. Admiring the soft clear skin of childhood, the long black silky lashes and the determined little chin, Kate's heart ached at the cruel removal of Darrel Brynton from this loving little family when he had so much to live for. Small wonder if Jean had found in Mark a father to take Darrel's place in Diana's life.

Beside the bed, sitting in a miniature armchair, sat Pulsatilla. It was a pretty little room, with wallpaper depicting Beatrix Potter characters, and pale pink curtains that stirred gently at the open casement window. The sun had set and the after-glow cast a soft warm light over the

Holiday Plans and Problems

room. In the garden, a blackbird was cheeping its last calls before going to roost. Quietly, Kate closed the door and returned to *Pride and Prejudice*.

Jean and Mark returned in good spirits soon after ten. Jean's eyes were shining and she looked happier than Kate had ever seen her before, transformed from the familiar, quiet, wan woman into someone much younger and prettier, with a charming animation that made it easy to understand the love she had inspired in Darrel Brynton as she enthused about the music they had heard. Then she reiterated her thanks to Kate with such gratitude that Kate had to say, "Any time, Jean, I'll be glad to oblige, especially if all the evenings are as peaceful as this has been. No sound from Diana all the evening."

"She's always been a good sleeper."

"If you're ready, Kate," said Mark.

"Yes. I seem to have mislaid my shoulder bag. Now where did I leave it? Don't bother, Jean. I'll have a scout round."

She tracked the bag down in the kitchen. As she came out, Mark's deep voice came clearly through the open sitting-room door.

"I can make the announcement, then, Jean, can I?"

"Yes. Just a simple ceremony, please, Mark."

"Of course. You're sure?"

"Quite sure. I won't let you down."

"It means a lot to hear you say that. I hardly dared hope. A turning-point for you, my dear."

"Yes. I can't ever tell you . . . " Jean's voice broke off as Kate closed the kitchen door firmly and made for the sitting-room with a decisive tread.

In the car, beside Mark, she was conscious of the cold calm of despair. So that was that. Any lingering hope that she might have misread the situation between Mark and Jean had now died. And during that short drive back to Dilford, she made an enormous effort to block out her own misery and think of those two. Surely she could be generous enough to wish them well. She had set Mark free nearly three years ago and had no claim on him. She had no right to feel aggrieved because he had found love elsewhere, to grudge him happiness. He had always been a good friend to her, had borne no grudge towards her for breaking their engagement.

"You're very quiet, Kate. Anything on your mind?"

"Nothing important. Just ruminating," she said, wondering if trying to screw herself up to a more noble outlook could be called ruminating. It felt more like self-laceration.

"You've been a great help to Jean these past months, Kate. She appreciates it, and so do I."

Jean, she thought. Always Jean. And immediately rapped herself for this lapse as they drew up at the shop.

"She needed help and I like her very much. But the thanks are mostly owing to you for coming to her aid, Mark. She deserves happiness now, and so do you," she added softly, and to her own surprise as well as his, she kissed his cheek before sliding out of the car and running round the shop to the flat entrance before he had time to say anything.

* * *

Driven by an aching restlessness, Kate took herself off for a long walk on Sunday, driving to a village at the foot of the South Downs and climbing up to follow the South Downs Way along the coast, tiring herself out, unable to drive from her mind the thought of Mark and Jean married and herself haunted by what might have been if she had not been so blind and foolish in the past. How could she escape such torments when she was tied to the Vermont family so securely by her affection for them and her business partnership with Valerie? How could she endure to stand by and witness their happiness? She had no answer when she arrived home, only a sort of bitter determination that it had to be endured, and with a good face. She would not cramp Mark's happiness by allowing him to guess for an instant how her feelings had changed, for she knew he was still fond of her and would be troubled by it. Nor would she allow the rest of the family to guess. She would say nothing to Valerie

Holiday Plans and Problems

of the confirmation of their surmise that there might be something serious between Mark and Jean. She would leave it to Mark to make the announcement in his own time, and then congratulate them with all the good will she could muster, and act as though delighted at this union of two friends. Perhaps, she thought bitterly, she had better ask Philippe for some lessons in acting.

On Monday, when the shop was closed, she busied herself with the stock records and accounts, determined to block any thoughts about Mark's engagement until he announced it. Valerie returned late that afternoon bubbling over with news.

"Evelyn telephoned yesterday to say that she and Hugh had rented a cottage in Yorkshire for the last week in August. It's got four bedrooms and a box room that makes a fifth, and she wants us all to join them. We were such a happy party last Christmas that she was sure we'd all have an enjoyable holiday together there. You, me, Mark, Jean. Evelyn's particularly keen on including Jean because Diana and Jeremy hit it off so well and will be company for each other. What do you think? I've never been to Yorkshire. I'd love to see the moors and dales."

"Sounds grand. But what about the shop?"

"We could close it for one week. We've earned a holiday, after all."

"I could stay and you go, Val."

"No. We both have a break or it's off for me, too. Do agree, Kate. It will make an odd number if you don't, and I think you need a holiday. Besides, I need you to help me endure dear Hugh."

"That settles it, then," said Kate, smiling, for she could not dampen the eager enthusiasm shining from Valerie's face although the prospect of being so close to Mark for a week and having to hide her feelings was daunting.

"Much as I love the shop, it will be grand to be free for a week, and explore the country, perhaps do some sketching," said Valerie.

"Have Mark and Jean agreed to come, too?"

"Mark wasn't all that keen. Said the family needed to be

taken in small doses and he wasn't one for communal holidays, but he thought it would be good for Jean to get away in a party, and if the idea appealed to her, we would need a second car and he said he'd provide it. All this was on the telephone, and we're all going home next weekend as it's Mother's birthday on Sunday and we'll have a conference then. And Mother specially wants you to come on Saturday evening with me and stay a couple of nights so that we can come back together on Monday. Mark will bring Jean over on Sunday morning and Hugh and Evelyn will join us then, too. Evelyn's going to bring a photograph of the cottage and tell us more about it."

Valerie stopped for breath, and Kate said, "We can rely on Evelyn to organise everything efficiently. She has your mother's gift for that. I hope she doesn't appoint Hugh as chief caterer, or we shall be on a very austere diet."

Thus it was that the Vermonts gathered at Greenhurst on the following Sunday, and Evelyn unfolded her plan, producing a brochure with a photograph of a picturesque long, low cottage with creeper-covered porch, set back from a lane behind flint walls.

"It's just here," said Evelyn, spreading a map on the table and pin-pointing the site. "Only half a mile from this village, where there are adequate shops. It has moors around it, is within easy reach of the dales and not too far from the sea."

"It sounds idyllic," said Jean.

"The last time I was in Yorkshire, it rained for a whole week without stopping," said Mark. "Given good weather, though, it's grand walking country. I'm not all that keen on do-it-yourself holidays, though."

"Don't be a wet blanket, Mark," said Evelyn.

"Especially with one's family," continued Mark.

"Do you good not to be waited on," said Valerie. "The trouble with you, Mark, is that you're treated like a little god at that Horticultural Station of yours. When I called in the other afternoon to leave that picture Dad had painted for you, I couldn't get past your secretary. What a dragon! 'I'm afraid the Director can't be interrupted now. He's in conference. Perhaps you would like to leave the parcel at the Director's house, Little Fenton, that red brick house beyond the glass-houses.' Back to the typewriter without another glance. Dismissed like a messenger boy, I staggered across to the house with the picture, only to meet your housekeeper. 'I'm sorry I can't stop now,' she said, eyeing me with suspicion. 'I'm just preparing dinner for the Director and two visitors from Holland. I want everything to be perfect this evening, including the salmon pâté which I'm working on now and which is the Director's favourite starter. So if you'll excuse me. Just leave the parcel on the hall table with any message, will you?' And before I could say anything, she'd disappeared into the back quarters. I was pretty fed up with this august Director by the time I'd finished, I can tell you."

Valerie, who was a good mimic, had evidently caught the clipped tart tones of the secretary and the slightly flustered voice of the housekeeper accurately enough to have Mark chuckling appreciatively.

"No wonder," went on Valerie, "that the Director needs pulling off his pedestal when he comes home. You come to Yorkshire and do a few humble chores for a change. I vote Mark does all the washing up."

"Well, we certainly shan't vote for you as our cook, Val. As a family, we don't go in for martyrdom," said Mark. "Personally, I foresee several snags in this scheme, but if a second car is needed, I'll provide it. Unless there are any other volunteers," he added drily, glancing at the other motorists in the party.

But there were no offers. Kate and Jean were not keen motorists, driving only for necessity, and nobody would put their lives in Valerie's hands.

"What do you think about Evelyn's scheme, Jean?" asked Mark. "Jeremy and Diana hit it off well and you could do with a change of scene."

"Do say yes, Jean," urged Evelyn. "The children will amuse each other, and we all get on so well together. We proved that last Christmas. I'm sure you'd enjoy it."

"So am I," replied Jean, smiling.

A Slender Thread

A beaming smile spread over Evelyn's face as she said,

"That's settled, then, and I don't want to hear any more talk of snags from you, Mark. We must all do our fair share of the chores, then they needn't weigh heavily on any one person. It's only a matter of catering, and I think the best way will be to split up the cooks among us and detail one assistant to each. That way we shan't get under each other's feet."

"Sounds like an army camp," observed Mark.

"The experienced cooks are Jean, Kate and myself. I suggest that Jean has Hugh to help – he's very handy – I'll have Val, and Kate can have Mark. If each pair takes on one day's catering in turn, that only means two days out of the week for each pair."

"Has Hugh made out a timetable?" asked Valerie wickedly, scenting his methodical hand in all this.

"Well, it was his idea, and a sensible one if we're not to find the good-natured ones saddled with all the chores and the shirkers none," said Evelyn, looking at Mark, who raised his eyebrows and looked heavenwards as though washing his hands of such a doubtful enterprise.

"It should work out all right, but I note that I've been saddled with the least promising assistant," said Kate.

"He'll probably turn out better than we think once he's brought his Director's mind down to a humbler level," said Valerie.

"Any decent restaurants within reach for a treat?" asked Mark imperturbably.

In the end, they finished their planning amicably.

"I'm sure you'll all have a lovely time," observed Marjorie Vermont.

"Grand walking and fishing country, the dales," said her husband.

"We could fit you both in if you'd like to join the party," said Mark, catching Kate's eye with the merest suspicion of a wink.

"Yes," said Kate, picking up his lead enthusiastically. "It would be splendid to have you with us. Do come, too."

But the expression of horror on Roland Vermont's face

and the struggle on his wife's face not to appear blighting were too much for Kate and their irreverent family.

"Well," said Roland sheepishly when the laughter had died down, "you know I hate long car journeys and it's not my kind of fishing there."

"Excuses won't help your hypocrisy," said Val. "What about you, Mother?"

"Having kept house for thirty-five years and reared three children, I don't intend to contemplate any holiday that involves domestic chores. A hotel with every service or nothing. For you young people, it's an entirely different matter."

"There you are. A kind of penitentiary now," said Mark.

During the whole of that birthday tea-party, Kate was on tenterhooks, expecting Mark to announce his engagement to Jean. It offered a golden opportunity, with all the family present, but it passed with lively chatter and no announcement from him.

To relieve her pent-up feelings, she took Crusoe for a walk across the heath after tea, accompanied by the children, who had both been on their best behaviour during the afternoon's discussion and now needed to let off steam. Their presence kept Kate from brooding too long on the fact that Mark would never have agreed to go on this Yorkshire holiday if it had not been for Jean. A fact confirmed by Valerie when the rest of the party had departed and she and Kate were alone in the garden that evening.

"It was obvious that Mark only agreed to come because of Jean. I'm beginning to think it's serious. What do you think, Kate?"

"I'm sure it is," said Kate, who was dead-heading a rose bed and did not look up as she spoke.

Valerie looked at her thoughtfully, but did not press her further, merely saying, "Well, I don't know why he has to be so secretive about it."

"Perhaps Jean wants a longer interval to elapse before making it official. Darrel died last September, I believe. Less than a year ago."

"That's the trouble. She still feels the loss, and I'm afraid

A Slender Thread

she'll only be marrying Mark for shelter. I don't think that's good enough.''

"If he cares deeply for her, it will be good enough," said Kate quietly, and exclaimed as a thorn from a Peace rose jabbed her finger.

While Valerie trundled the wheelbarrow away to the compost heap at the end of the garden to dispose of the weeds she had removed from the bed, Kate cupped a velvety red rose in her hands and studied it with a mangled feeling of pain that suddenly seemed unbearable. But bearable and hidden it must be. The holiday in prospect would be a severe test, her pleasure at the thought of Mark's presence there in conflict with the torment of seeing him and Jean together and the necessity to hide from all of them her distress. Most difficult of all would be hiding her true feelings from Mark, who knew her so well.

The sun had set and the grass was damp with dew. The fragrance of the roses hung on the air. There was little birdsong, just a piping blackbird and a snatch of song from a robin, who had turned up while Valerie was weeding, anxious to seize any titbits from the newly disturbed earth. It was so peaceful there in the shadowy garden that Kate felt her own turbulent thoughts were quite out of place, but they were too insistent to be dismissed.

13
Squalls

When in after years Kate looked back on that Yorkshire holiday, she likened it to being tossed about in a small boat on a very rough sea, with short intervals of calm to encourage her to endure it.

The day was fine when they set out, Valerie travelling with Evelyn, Hugh and Jeremy, and Mark taking Jean, Diana and Kate. Thundery weather during the previous week had cleared the air and signalled the end of that long heat wave, but the sun shone brightly in a blue sky with puffy white clouds chasing across it before a lively southwest wind as they travelled north. Both cars made an early start, but not early enough, for they found heavy traffic most of the way.

Kate sat beside Mark, while Jean read a story to Diana in the back. After the first hour, caught in a traffic hold-up, Mark handed a map to Kate and they worked out a route using the byways.

"I've had enough of this," he said as he turned off the motorway.

"I wonder how Hugh's faring," said Kate.

"Better, perhaps, starting from Surrey. He hoped to get moving about six o'clock this morning and may have avoided the bottlenecks we've hit."

He was an easy, relaxed driver, but not a chatty one, and Kate concentrated on the map. They stopped for lunch at a country hotel which looked attractive from the outside, with its creeper-covered walls and tubs of geraniums, but seemed faded and dusty within. There were only two other people in the large, rather dark dining-room, and the elderly waiter produced a dingy menu with a resigned air as though daring them to have any high expectations. After some nondescript soup, roast beef which had all too obviously been warmed up and now swam in gravy, they refused the apple pie and finished with some tasteless cheese and weak instant coffee.

"Well, we shall do better than that with our own catering," said Kate when they emerged into the sunshine.

"I hope so. Sorry about that. A bad choice," said Mark.

"The ice cream was nice," said Diana, hopping round the tubs of geraniums.

They arrived at the cottage just half an hour after Hugh, their spirits improved by the beauty of the moors on the last stretch of their journey. Kate sniffed the spicy scent of the heather and stretched her limbs with pleasure.

"This smells good and looks good," she added, as they surveyed the stone cottage which nestled in a fold of the foothills of the moors. Behind its low flint wall, the garden was bright with sunflowers, marigolds and snapdragons.

Evelyn stood in the doorway, beaming at them.

"Tea's ready," she said. "Welcome to our cottage."

The interior of the cottage matched the charm of its exterior with its low beamed ceilings, exposed timber and stonework, large stone fireplace and warm chintz furnishings. Evelyn, anxious for the success of her enterprise, had produced a tempting tea of sandwiches, scones, honey, jam and fruit cake set out on a dark oak refectory table in a dining-room flooded with the mellow light of the late afternoon sun. It could not have been a better start to the holiday.

They walked up the hill behind the cottage that evening to watch the sun set over the folds of the moors spread out before them, the heather turning from pink to deep purple beneath a rose-streaked sky in the afterglow. Kate leaned on a low stone wall after the others returned, wanting to soak in the peace and quietness and beauty of that empty landscape.

Squalls

She did not notice Mark turning back until he leaned on the wall beside her.

"You seem to have been very elusive lately. I haven't been able to catch you alone since that surprisingly fond farewell about a month ago, after your baby-sitting stint."

"No? Well, the shop keeps me very busy."

They were silent for a few moments. It was true, she had avoided being alone with him since the devastating discovery of his commitment to Jean and her own love for him. She felt an odd constraint in his presence now, the effort to hide the tumult of her feelings blocking the old easy comradeship.

"You know, I found that dismissal rather disconcerting. Not my bracing Kate at all. More like a sad, consoling pat on the shoulder for an unlucky victim of fate."

So much for trying to be noble, thought Kate, but all she said was,

"The heat must have melted me."

"You're not still fretting over Philippe, are you?"

"No. I haven't given him a thought for weeks."

"Well, I'm glad of that, but I feel that something's biting you. To be candid, I find you a bit puzzling these days, and that's a new experience. Is anything wrong, Kate? You know you can turn to me for any kind of help."

Was anything wrong? Everything was wrong, she thought sadly. And he was the last person she could tell. With an enormous effort she managed to raise a smile and say lightly, "Thank you, Mark. I do know that, but really, there's no problem. Isn't that a kestrel?"

"Too far to be sure without binoculars. I think you're hedging, Kate. But if you think it's none of my business, O.K. I suspect you haven't come out of your romantic dreams about Philippe, though, and if so, I've very little sympathy. Romantic dreams are for teenagers," he concluded coldly, and left her to go after the rest of the party.

It was not a propitious end to the day, and she stayed on to watch the last pink glow fade from the sky, but failed to

119

recapture the tranquil mood of the evening, and felt tempted to rest her head on the wall and cry her heart out.

* * *

She woke next morning to the sound of rain drumming on the window and a strong wind blowing the curtains. Shutting the window, she saw only wet mist where the moors must be and an unbroken grey sky.

The rain poured relentlessly down all that day and the next. They passed the time playing Scrabble, going on car expeditions when all they could do was nose their way cautiously through thick wet mists, doing crossword puzzles, and jig-saw puzzles with the children, while those antisocial enough retired to another room with a book, reading being difficult to concentrate on in the communal living-room. Their one consolation was the large open fire on which they burned the logs abundantly provided.

Nerves were getting frayed on the third day, which differed only from the first two by the appearance now and again of patches of blue sky among the scurrying clouds and a clearing of the mist, the rain coming in squalls.

"I shall go mad if I can't get away from Hugh," said Valerie half way through the morning. "He's just been instructing me on the best way to peel a pear. Took it right out of my hand just as I was hacking it about. I like it hacked about in chunks."

Valerie, whose happy-go-lucky nature found her pedantic brother-in-law more trying than most, was pink with indignation as she cornered Kate in the hall.

"Let's brave the weather and go out," said Kate.

"I've got a better idea. Why don't we go to the coast and have a swim? After all, rain doesn't matter when you're in the sea. I'll ask Mark if he'll drive us. Otherwise, we'll take one of the cars ourselves."

Mark agreed to take his car, and no other members of the party finding the prospect of a swim on a chilly wet day tempting, the three of them stowed towels and swimming suits in the boot of the car and set off. It was just under an

Squalls

hour's drive to the coast, and they found a sandy cove not far from Scarborough. They also found a south-west gale blowing and mountainous waves breaking on the shore. Mark and Kate were strong swimmers, Valerie less so, but Mark had no hesitation in shouting,

"No go. It would be foolhardly."

And eyeing the walls of green water that reared and thundered up the beach in a seething mass of surf, Kate and Valerie agreed. It had stopped raining, but the sky was a leaden grey and the sea streaked with white foam far out. Only the screech of gulls as they flew before the wind penetrated the booming of the waves and the roar of the gale which buffeted them as they stood there. Exhilarated by the sheer boisterousness of the scene, they walked along the beach, the wind half blowing them along, and paused for breath in the shelter of a jutting peninsula of cliff.

The return journey was less exhilarating, for as well as the difficulty of fighting their way against the wind, sand blew against their faces, and Kate and Valerie huddled inside the hoods of their anoraks exposing as little as possible, while Mark, who was bare-headed, turned up the collar of his duffle coat and wound a scarf round the bottom half of his face. They were glad to get back to the car and survey the ferocious mood of nature from its shelter. Valerie and Kate nipped in quickly, but Mark spent a few minutes trying to remove some of the salt from the windscreen. Watching him, Kate saw him with fresh eyes, not as the friend of so many years but as other women saw him, as Jean saw him. A lean face, tanned by the abundant sunshine of the summer, thick black hair blowing across his forehead. Unmistakably a man of some authority with a firm assurance which she had often vainly rebelled against in the past. A face that revealed little of his emotions, but could soften with an eye-creasing charm when he laughed. And the deep ache which she felt for him was of an intensity she had never known before.

They stopped at an inn for a snack lunch on the way back, by which time it was raining again with a ferocity that the windscreen wipers could scarcely cope with.

A Slender Thread

"Somebody has a grudge against the land," observed Valerie mournfully.

* * *

Kate, who was doing the catering stint the next day, decided to lift their spirits by preparing a special dinner for the evening. The rest of the party, except Valerie, bundled into Mark's car and went off to York for the day, since Hugh and Jeremy wanted to see the Railway Museum there and Mark and Jean wanted to visit York Minster and walk round the old walls of the city.

"I'll be back in time to give you a hand this evening, Kate," said Mark. "Sure you won't come? We can take the other car as well."

"Not to worry. Valerie and I are going to do the shopping in the village and then go for a ramble if the weather holds."

"Squalls was the weather forecast."

She watched them drive off, Jean in the front with Mark, Evelyn, Hugh and the children in the back. Diana waved to them as they went by.

"It will be rather nice to have a quiet day to ourselves. We'll explore that river path when we get back from shopping. I'd like to do some sketching before we go back. There's actually a gleam of sunshine getting through up there," added Valerie, peering up at the mottled sky.

And for Kate, too, there was a certain relief in being alone with Valerie, the easiest of companions, for she was aware of a growing tension between herself and Mark. He had probably been annoyed by her rejection of his offer of help on the evening of their arrival, and irritated by what he interpreted as her fretting after Philippe. And she was finding her nerves stretched by the effort to hide her true feelings from him.

They came back from the village laden with chicken, mushrooms, runner beans, two melons, fresh fruit, cheese and two bottles of wine, remembering just in time to add a bottle of mineral water for Hugh.

"We'll start with melon, follow with a chicken casserole, and have a choice of a French apple tart or fresh fruit salad for dessert. Cheese to finish if desired," said Kate.

"Sounds good, but do you want to do all that cooking? It is a holiday, after all," said Valerie, not an enthusiastic cook herself.

"It will cheer us all up, and with dinner not until eight o'clock, after the children are in bed, I shan't need to start cooking early. We shall have the day free."

With their purchases stowed away, they took some biscuits and cheese and an apple apiece in their pockets and set off. Kate viewed the ominous clouds rising behind the high line of the moor with some misgivings, but a fitful sun played about the river valley and Valerie enthused about the light. They stopped at the field next to their cottage to have a few words with the resident donkey, a diminutive animal, morosely surveying the world over a five-barred gate. They each gave him half an apple and ate the other half themselves. The donkey had dark eyes fringed with long lashes, and appeared to enjoy their presence, for, having demolished the apple, he walked alongside them inside the stone wall until they reached the river path and left the field behind.

The river was running fast, fed by the rains, creating miniature waterfalls over the rocks, sparkling in the fitful sunshine. Already the trees and bushes along its banks were showing the tints of autumn, and the mountain ash trees carried glowing clusters of berries. Valerie's efforts to sketch a stone bridge overhung by a contorted alder were interrupted by a fierce squall which had them crouching under a holly tree. Their lunch was likewise eaten whilst sheltering from another squall. When the squalls merged into longer periods of rain, they turned back and arrived at the cottage in time for an early tea, after which Kate began preparations for dinner.

"If I get the tart done now, we can have it cold. It's just as good, hot or cold."

"I'll do the fruit salad," said Valerie. "I wonder what time the others will get back."

A Slender Thread

"They planned to have tea in York. Be back about six, according to Evelyn."

The York party arrived rather sooner than expected, just as Kate surveyed with satisfaction the neat, thin slices of apple carefully arranged on her pastry base and put the tart into the oven.

"We got caught in a cloud burst," said Jean, "getting from the tea shop to the car."

"And someone in the car park had hit the back of our car and dented one wing and broken a rear light," added Hugh. "But the Railway Museum was excellent. Fascinating."

They dispersed to get into dry clothes, leaving Valerie and Kate alone in the kitchen. Through the kitchen window they could see Mark in the lane, examining the back of the car.

"Not the happiest of expressions," observed Valerie. "I expect he would have preferred it alone with Jean. I'll ask him," she added in a mischievous mood.

"I wouldn't advise it. Mark in an east wind mood is not a good subject for teasing. That fruit salad looks good enough to be framed."

Perversely, the sun was shining brightly from a clear sky as Valerie strolled down the front path to the lane. She returned some minutes later, flushed and almost in tears. Kate looked at her in astonishment, for Valerie had the sunniest of natures, seldom ruffled or distressed.

"What's the matter, Val?"

"Mark. Bit my head off. Accused me, us, of objectionable gossip which could do a lot of harm. He's never spoken to me like that before. All because of a little chivvying about Jean."

Valerie's lip quivered, and Kate put a sympathetic hand on her shoulder, her anger with Mark boiling up.

"He's going to have a few words with you, too," went on Valerie. "I'm sorry, Kate. I said you had no doubts about their involvement with each other, either. That you were sure there was a secret engagement. I wish I hadn't brought you into it."

"Not to worry. If he has to be so secretive, that's no

excuse for being so brutal when he's found out. I'm going to have a few words with *him*," added Kate as Valerie ran out of the room in tears.

He must have been savage indeed to have upset Valerie so much. She was very fond of her brother and they had always been good friends. His conduct was shameful and she would tell him so. All the pent up frustrations and unhappiness of the past weeks welled up into a dangerous anger as she marched down the path to the lane where Mark was still trying to effect some repair. He straightened up when he saw her, his face as bleak as an arctic winter.

"How could you upset Valerie so, Mark? To be so cruel to anyone as good-natured as your sister is inexcusable."

"And gossip that could do untold harm is inexcusable. Gossip set up by you, I gather."

"No gossip," she snapped. "Nothing has gone beyond Valerie and me. And not gossip, but facts. Anyone would think we'd accused you of murder, the way you're behaving. Is it so unnatural for your family to be interested in your personal affairs?"

"Not facts. Gossip," he said, ignoring her question. "Your foolish, romantic fantasies spill over to other people's affairs as well as your own. Will you never grow up?"

This acted like a match to brushwood, and all restraint left her.

"You've become an autocratic bully, Mark, who doesn't deserve the family he's got. You order your minions about in your job and think you can keep everybody else in line. You're secretive and won't allow anybody to raise even a question into your lordly affairs."

"You've lost your temper, Kate."

"You're dead right. That's why you can listen to a few more home truths. Not only are you bossy, secretive and unkind, but you think that you have the wonderful gift of seeing exactly what is in the mind of others. You know it all. A walking X-ray machine."

He surveyed her calmly. That was the worst of fighting Mark. He never lost control. His voice was cold.

"Have you finished?"

A Slender Thread

"No. Please apologise to Valerie for your brutal behaviour. If you want to vent your quite unjustified anger on anybody, it's me. I confirmed her guess about you and Jean. That appears to have been a crime in your eyes. So be it. But you owe your sister an apology."

"Perhaps. I can see how you fed her with your romantic imagination. I'll make amends with Val. You, I'll put right some other time when you're in a more rational frame of mind."

"I'm perfectly rational. Have your say now."

"If you could see your face, rational would not be the word to spring to mind. It's been a long day, we all got soaked, York was packed, the car parks were all full, and the kids bickered all the way home, to say nothing of the damage to the car. Enough is enough. We'll finish this row some other time, Kate. Meanwhile, may I have your word that you won't spread this gossip about Jean and me to another soul? It could cause great embarrassment and distress."

"Never fear. I wash my hands of you and your secret affairs," said Kate coldly, but spoilt the dignity of this reply with an anguished cry. "My tart!"

And she rushed back to the kitchen leaving Mark gazing after her in angry astonishment. In the doorway to the kitchen, she bumped into Valerie, red-eyed but torn between laughter and tears as she flapped a weak hand towards the kitchen. Over her shoulder, Kate saw the donkey withdraw his nose from the bowl of fruit salad and gaze at her steadily with juice dripping from his mouth. An ominous smell of burning came from the cooker. With another anguished cry, Kate seized a cloth and withdrew a blackened mess from the oven.

"The donkey," gasped Valerie, "came round the back. The door was open."

Mark joined them in time to see Kate cajoling the donkey from the front, Valerie pushing from the back in a vain endeavour to get him through the side door into the garden, a smoking dish of charred remains on the table and a slippery trail of fruit salad on the floor. He raised his arms to heaven.

Squalls

"There's a curse on this holiday. Move over, Val. I'll shift him."

And with a smart smack on his rump and a helping hand, Mark induced the animal to leave the fruits of the kitchen for the less rewarding fruits of the field.

"Someone must have left that field gate open. I'd better get him back there," said Mark. "I'm sorry I blew my top just now, Val. It's been a trying day, but that's no excuse. You were led astray by Kate, no doubt. There's no truth in your belief that there's anything more than friendship between Jean and me. Can we forget it now?"

"Right," said Valerie.

Mark looked at her keenly, then put an arm round her shoulder.

"I'm truly sorry, Val. Can I make amends by standing you a dinner at the Royal Swan when we get home? I admit I was in a filthy temper."

"All right. I shall choose all the most expensive items," said Valerie, recovering.

"You do that. Now I'd better get that donkey back home before another calamity strikes us."

He came into the kitchen a little later, having changed into a tweed suit.

"I'm supposed to be your assistant, Kate. What can I do?"

Kate, slicing beans, said,

"Nothing, thank you. Everything's organised."

"Can I take on that job?"

"I wouldn't like to trouble you, and anyway, I prefer the kitchen to myself."

"As you wish," he said icily, and left her.

In spite of the mishaps, the dinner that night was voted a great success. The melon was deliciously ripe, the casserole excellent, and even Hugh was tempted by the Stilton cheese, although normally he would have resisted this because of its high fat content. And the wine had the desired effect of lifting their spirits, at least on the surface, thought Kate, as she looked round the table. But what were they really thinking beneath the lively chatter and laughter? Jean was

A Slender Thread

smiling at something Mark was saying to her. She had been transformed lately from the woebegone figure of the early months of the year. Her cheeks had filled out, her tawny eyes were unshadowed, her sensitive mouth curved more often now into a warm smile. An easy face to love. Had she backed away from that announcement she had agreed to? Was that the reason for Mark's grim mood? Perhaps she had asked for more time to elapse between the loss of her husband and a second marriage. That would account for Mark's dismay at the possibility of any premature leakage of the news. It would embarrass Jean, make it seem as though he was forcing her hand. Always, his thought was for Jean now. To spare her feelings. To help her. The rest of them could go hang.

She turned her eyes to the object of her anger, sipping his wine, apparently at ease. Not troubled, it seemed, by having subjected Valerie and herself to a verbal assault that was both cruel and unjustified. "Will you never grow up?" She was still burning at the injustice of those words. Like Valerie, she had never experienced the rough edge of his tongue. And like Valerie, was deeply wounded by it, although her reaction was anger rather than tears. But deep down, it hurt.

Next to Mark, Evelyn was telling Valerie about Queen Victoria's special railway coach on view at the York museum. She must be feeling a little disappointed about this holiday venture which the weather had spoiled, but if so, she had never lost her cheerful manner and practical approach to all problems. Beside her, Hugh was buttering a biscuit with finicky precision, studying it through his horn rimmed spectacles as though measuring every calorie. No use trying to read Hugh's thoughts. They were not on the same wave length as hers. She sighed, and found Mark's eyes on her. She concentrated on her plate. For the rest of the holiday she would be formally polite to him, and leave him severely alone when possible. But as with most of the plans for that holiday, this one, too, went awry.

14
Misadventure

The next day, the climate relented and they were greeted at breakfast by sunshine and a cloudless sky, with a cool breeze blowing. The party split into two. Jean and Evelyn chose to drive to a mill some twenty miles away to see some tweeds being woven, and buy skirts if they pleased them. The others chose to drive to one of the loveliest dales in the area and explore it on foot. Diana, attached to Jeremy, chose to go with the latter party. It occurred to Kate that Jeremy was tiring a little of his companion. The year's difference in their age seemed more marked now, for Jeremy was a wiry, energetic boy who sometimes left the toiling Diana behind. However, clad in bright blue dungarees over a pink woollen jumper, clutching Pulsatilla, Diana refused to be put off and clambered into the back of Mark's car after a rather sulky Jeremy.

Bumping down a rough track, Mark found a flat grassy space a few yards from the river for their base. The river was wide and deep at that point, and overhung by tall trees. Its course wound through steep wooded slopes, which Valerie set about exploring for wild flowers, aided by Kate, who politely refused Mark's suggestion of a walk upstream. He responded to this refusal with a cool nod and went off on his own. Later, far below them, Kate saw Hugh and the children peering into the water for signs of life.

"I bet Hugh's instructing them on the difference between a trout and a carp," said Valerie. "Look, I believe that's a Lady's Tresses orchid."

Fired by this discovery, they went deeper into the woods, absorbed until lunch-time.

After their picnic lunch, Valerie decided to soak up some of the sun before resuming her search for wild flowers in the woods, and stretched herself out on a rug by the car. Hugh took himself off to a perch on some higher ground behind the car, binoculars slung around his neck, intent on bird-watching.

Mark went across to Kate, who was sitting on the river bank looking for trout, and said, "Come to the other side of the river, Kate. I want to talk to you. There's a footpath that looks inviting."

"I've nothing to say to you, Mark."

"You owe me an explanation for your idiotic assumptions about Jean and me. Come on. You talked about facts. Enlighten me."

"I don't intend to have the first sunny day we've had here spoiled by continuing that row. It's finished, as far as I'm concerned. Your affairs are your own secret."

He took her arm in a grip that hurt, pulled her to her feet and said quietly,

"I've a right to an explanation when gossip is spread that could cause mischief, and I'm going to have it. I presume you don't want to engage in a brawl."

And keeping her arm in an iron grip, he walked her across the bridge and up a steeply climbing footpath through the woods on the other side of the river. She shook herself free and climbed up ahead of him in silent anger. Close on her heels, he drew her to a halt in a clearing and said,

"Now, let's have it."

She turned away from him, rubbing her arm, trying to control her anger. Below them, the river sparkled in the sunshine, and the car windscreen winked back at them. Valerie's red trousers were visible on the low slope of the woods opposite them. She had resumed her wild-flower search. Hugh had his binoculars trained downstream. The grassy clearing round the car was emerald green, and on it two small figures appeared to be having a slight altercation. Kate saw Diana stamp her foot, then run after Jeremy, who seemed bent on getting away on his own. He turned as she tugged at his jersey, snatched the doll away from her and threw it high into the tree beside them. Then, as Diana put her hands up to her face in dismay, he ran off.

"Oh no!" Kate exclaimed as she saw Diana start to climb the tree, her small legs finding it difficult to reach footholds. Pulsatilla was dangling high above her on a branch overhanging the river.

Mark followed Kate's gaze. They were too high up for their voices to carry with any warning, and Hugh was unsighted.

"Come on," said Mark, and they ran back down the path keeping one eye on the child who was now inching her way towards the doll. Mark yelled to her to go back just as she put a hand out to the doll, lost her balance and fell into the river below. Kate cried out in horror.

"She'll drown. It's deep water and she can't swim."

Hugh, alerted by Mark's shout and the cry from Diana as she fell, threw his binoculars down, stood up and immediately raced to the river and waded in.

"He can't swim," said Mark, then saved his breath as they raced down the path.

Hugh, with a kind of dog paddle, had somehow reached Diana, who was clutching some twigs at the end of a slender branch which swept the water, and was awash when Hugh grabbed her. He managed to hoist her further along the branch and hold her there, treading water and struggling to keep afloat.

"Go in from the bridge, Kate," said Mark.

"I'll go for Diana," she gasped. "You get to Hugh. He's going under."

"Sure you can handle Diana?"

"Yes," she said, and they dived off the bridge together.

Kate reached Diana just as the branch was going under with her weight, and was thankful that the little girl was too stunned by the shock to struggle, and only whimpered as Kate took her in tow and soothed her, herself in an anguished state of fear as the water behind her showed no signs of either Hugh or Mark. Those few terrible moments seemed a lifetime before Mark's head emerged, gasping and spluttering, with Hugh, limp and seemingly unconscious in his grasp.

Valerie, alerted by the cries, came racing down from the woods and reached the river bank in time to help Kate out.

"Dry towels in the boot of the car," Kate gasped. "Get her into my sweater . . . on the bridge . . . Must get back to help Mark."

Mark, looking exhausted, was within his depth now, and stood, coughing and gasping, holding Hugh, who was still inert. Kate reached him and took one of Hugh's arms round her neck while Mark took the other, and together they got him out on to the bank.

"Diana all right?"

"Yes. Val's taken her to the car."

"Well done."

He had turned Hugh over and was applying artificial respiration. After a few moments, he said, "It's all right. He's responding. Go and get out of those wet clothes, Kate."

"Your hand's bleeding."

"Is it? I had a job to get him free from roots and weed. All right, Hugh," he added and lifted him so that Hugh's thin frame was doubled over to aid the release of water from his lungs.

As he came round, Kate found herself shaking. It had all happened so quickly. With the danger past, strength seemed to drain from her. She felt Mark's arms round her shoulders.

"Hold on. I can't lose my helper now."

"You were down so long. I thought you'd both gone."

He held her for a moment, then released her and said, "Get into your swimming gear. It's still in the boot of the car. Tell Val to round up Jeremy. We'd better get Diana and Hugh back as soon as possible."

Valerie came running to them, and gasped with relief when she saw Hugh sitting up, head bent, coughing and moaning a little.

"Diana's recovered. Wants her mother. But refuses to

Misadventure

leave that confounded doll," said Valerie, and was about to climb the tree when Mark pulled her back.

"Let me. I refuse to pull another body out of the river. Find Jeremy, Val. I want to get Hugh back quickly."

It was a subdued party in the car. Kate sat in the back, with Diana half asleep on her lap clasping Pulsatilla. Hugh, swathed in a towel and an old travelling rug, was propped up beside her, white but fully conscious. Jeremy, silent and scared by the consequences of his impulsive action, crouched on the edge of the seat between them. It was warm in the car, with the heater working, and the swimming suits and towels left in the boot of the car since their trip to the coast had enabled them to change from their wet clothes.

Kate, her eyes on Mark's tousled damp hair, was reliving those terrible moments when she thought he and Hugh were lost. Foolish, really, because Mark was a strong swimmer, but he had been under an uncomfortably long time, and could have been trapped, as Hugh was. It was chilling to think that life could be perched on such a knife edge. One moment, a happy picnic party, the next, tragedy. Only Hugh's bravery had saved Diana, for she and Mark had been too far off to get to her after she fell. And only Mark's strength had saved Hugh. And she felt cold at the thought that they had so nearly had to return to the cottage and tell Evelyn and Jean of their loss. And how could they ever have faced them with that news?

The other car was already parked behind the cottage when Mark drew up. Jean was picking some roses in the garden, and waved to them.

Diana was first out of the car. With Kate's pale blue sweater reaching nearly to her ankles, the sleeves falling down over her hands, she ran to Jean, saying,

"I felled in the water, Mummy, and Pulsatilla lost her hat."

Jean clasped her and looked at Mark with wide eyes as he told her briefly what had happened. Then Evelyn, having caught a glimpse of Hugh through the window, ran out, her face white.

"What's happened? Hugh, my dear!"

A Slender Thread

Hugh, staggering a little, gave his wife a smile and said with a reassuring gentleness that caught at Kate's throat, "Nothing to worry about, my love. A cold dip. Mark fished me out. I've lost my specs."

Evelyn took him in her arms for a moment, then released him, recovered herself, and took things in hand with her usual brisk confidence, ushering them indoors with talk of hot drinks and hot baths.

Staying behind the others to fish the wet clothes out of the boot, Kate found Mark beside her. She still felt sick and shaky. Delayed shock, she thought, trying to control her hands. He took the wet things from her, and said gently, "It's all right, dear. Come and get a cup of tea inside you. It's all right."

"But it so nearly wasn't, Mark."

"I know."

"Hugh was so brave. He couldn't swim. Didn't hesitate. I'll never forget it. And but for you, he would have drowned."

"And all for a doll," said Mark with a twisted smile. "Fate plays nasty tricks with our lives. Come on. Be thankful. I couldn't have saved Hugh if I hadn't had you to rely on for Diana. We've one more day to this holiday. I hope we survive it."

And they went in together.

That evening, gathered round the log fire, for the evening had about it the chill of autumn, they were in reflective mood. Hugh, who had emerged from a couple of hours sleep, pale but more or less recovered, looked oddly naked without his heavy horn-rimmed spectacles, lost in the river. His face looked younger, more vulnerable, perhaps because he was short-sighted and had to peer at everything. There were things about that day she would never forget, Kate thought, and one of them was the smile Hugh had given his wife and the tenderness between them. Never again would she wonder why Evelyn had married him, and never again would she be impatient with his ways. He could put her right in everything she did in future, and she would accept his corrections with a smile.

Somehow, that day had brought them all closer together. The strains that had been building up had melted away. A mood of thankfulness and mutual affection hung over them all as Jean tuned the radio set to a Mozart concert, and that happiest of composers seemed to match their mood. They sat on in the firelight, quiet and relaxed; while the flames cast a flickering pattern across the white walls.

Mark's face was in shadow as he leaned back in his armchair, long legs stretched before him. Their quarrel of the previous day now seemed unreal, childish. They had acted instinctively as a team that afternoon, she and Mark. No division between them. Whatever his feelings towards Jean, she had his affection and respect. He had relied on her, had confidence in her. And that was unchangeable, whatever his plans for the future. And with that, she could, if she had to, be content.

15
Getting It Straight

Mark sought Kate out in the garden the next morning. Once again, the sun was shining from a clear sky.

"Val's going to spend the day sketching down the river. Wants to finish the stone bridge. The others have opted for a quiet day here. Hugh's still a bit wobbly. I'd like to take the car and have the day on the moors with you. We seem to have crossed our lines badly these past months. I want to try to straighten them out. Will you come?"

"Yes."

Their attention was drawn to Diana, who had emerged from the cottage with a large book under her arm. That morning she was wearing bright green dungarees with a green and white checked blouse under them.

"No ill effects there from yesterday, thank goodness," observed Kate.

"No. She's a sturdy little soul. Jeremy looks a bit sheepish," added Mark, as the boy followed Diana, tossing a ball. "Quailing, no doubt, from the lecture Hugh gave him."

They watched as Jeremy approached Diana and invited her to play with him. Diana subjected him to a long, grave examination, then, without a word, turned away, walked to the seat at the end of the garden, climbed on it and opened her book. Jeremy stared after her, shrugged his shoulders and ran off, vaulting the low stone wall into the field beyond.

"I've not seen any cooler snubs than that," said Mark, amused. "The end of a beautiful friendship, I fear."

"It's a disillusioning world," said Kate.

"I've seen Darrel use just the same technique with trainees guilty of sloppy work. The long, silent inspection. Most unnerving. His daughter is uncannily like him. But it's time we turned our attention to our own tangles."

They took a packed lunch and set out across the rolling, purple moors. After a short distance, Mark parked the car in a lay-by, and they walked, striking out across the heather. It was not until they stopped to rest by the side of a stream that he brought up the subject that had been occupying the thoughts of both of them.

"About Jean, Kate. I really can't understand why you should have thought I was going to marry her. It's not as though I didn't explain to you why I had to look after her when Darrel died. You asked me, and I told you. Since then, you've befriended her and must have seen for yourself that she is still wedded to Darrel. He still lives in her heart and mind to the exclusion of anybody else. Surely you must have sensed that."

"She could need you for support."

"Never, except as a friend. The idea of marrying anybody else would be unthinkable to her. I doubt whether she will ever marry again. Certainly not for a long, long time. There was never any question of more than friendship between us. A promise I'd made to Darrel."

"Friendship can turn to love."

"What grounds have you for believing that, then?"

"I saw Jean in your arms that evening I came to the cottage with the present for Diana's birthday. In the garden. You didn't hear or see me. I went away for a bit. Came back later."

Mark plucked a piece of heather and fingered it thoughtfully.

"I remember. Jean had been looking at old snapshots. They had brought it all back. The loss. The grief. When she saw me coming down the garden, she ran to me and just collapsed in a hopeless fit of crying. I was merely a shoulder to lean on."

"The evening I came to the cottage to baby-sit," said Kate jerkily. "I overheard, couldn't help overhearing, your talk of a simple ceremony . . . making an announcement . . . a turning point for Jean. You sounded so happy. What else could it mean?''

Mark threw away the piece of heather and raised his hands as though in helpless protest at the tricks of fate.

"Good grief! I see what you mean. The simple ceremony was referring to the opening of a new enlarged library at the Station which we are naming after Darrel. It was his scheme. I wanted Jean to open it. She's had long connections with the Station. Her father worked for us and was a brilliant scientist, did some good work in the labs when Darrel was only a junior, long before my time. It's played a big part in her life. So it seemed specially fitting that she should perform the opening ceremony, but I scarcely dared hope she would agree. She hasn't been near the Station since Darrel's death. But that night, at the concert, she was different. Seemed to have a hold on life again. When I broached it she agreed, and I was delighted. I knew she'd come through then, and that my job of keeping her afloat had ended successfully. The opening ceremony will be the week after next, to coincide with our annual open day. You know about that.''

"Yes. Val told me about it. Heavens, what a mix-up!''

"There was no secret about it. I'd have told you about it, but you were in an odd mood when I drove you home. And I was completely foxed by your sad, fond farewell. If you were supposed to be congratulating me on a happy event, it wasn't a very good effort. Felt more like a condolence. I was completely thrown by it.''

"So much for trying to be noble.''

"Not your line. I felt all at sea with you. A very disconcerting experience. I prefer the fists up, with which I'm familiar. Not that I want any repetition of our last bout.''

"We both said things then that are best forgotten. I was furious with you for laying into Val, and because of all the frustrations and speculations. All your thoughts were for Jean. All the time. To a greater extent than friendship would account for.''

"Perhaps I didn't explain the situation fully enough when

you asked me that time. It was a painful experience, not one I wanted to talk about. I shan't ever forget that night when Darrel was dying. He'd refused pain-killing drugs to keep his mind clear when he saw me. He was terribly injured. Bandaged and cradled. In pain all the time he dragged the words out. He told me how vulnerable Jean was, how close they were. She'd had an unhappy childhood, a tragedy with the man she was engaged to before Darrel, and her sensitive nature had always shrunk from the harshness of life. He said she was not without grit, but she would need a supporting hand for the first months. Otherwise, he was afraid for her. She knew and trusted me. Would I look after her until she found her feet? My promise seemed to relieve him enormously. I was glad to give it. He was my very good friend.

"Jean came in afterwards, and stayed with him until he died early the next morning. And when it was all over, she went to pieces. She had farmed Diana out with friends, and was slow in sending for her. At one time, I feared she might do something desperate. But in the end, she weathered it, as you know. You helped there, too. That's why I was so pleased that night. Her acceptance of our invitation to her to open the library marked a new beginning for her. And that's why I was so angry at the thought of gossip about us that would have distressed her, and might have set her back. Can you understand now why I had to devote myself to her and not to my girl, who was away with another lover, anyway?"

"Yes. Darrel would be grateful to you."

"I was in his debt. I don't think I'd want to live through this year again, though. I inherited his job before I was really ready for it, had Jean to care for, and saw the only girl I've ever wanted to marry fall in love with my cousin. I reached an all time low when Madeleine attacked you at Val's birthday party and Pamela stuck her claws in."

"Not pretty."

"Not pretty at all. Now it's time you did some explaining. Philippe. It went wrong? It seemed to me that you were unhappy this summer."

"Not about that. Yes, it went wrong. After that nightmare party, I went to Phil for an explanation. It wasn't me that weekend. He was using me as a cover up. I can't give details, as Phil would only come clean if I promised to keep it to myself. But, briefly, it would have embarrassed him if the name of the married woman in question had come out, could have hindered his career.''

"How like Phil! But there could never have been any future in it, Kate. Phil takes his love affairs lightly. Always has. I knew you'd get hurt.''

"Hurt? Yes, up to a point. It's always painful to have one's dreams broken, even though they were childish, romantic dreams nursed for too long. And it was humiliating, to be used. But I was in love with a myth. A figment of my imagination who did not exist. What cured me completely was the realisation that Phil had actually enjoyed pulling wool over everybody's eyes. At the party he gave, he acted my lover so enthusiastically that nobody could have been in doubt about it. Even hoodwinked Madeleine, too, so that she added her disapproval of the affair to add authenticity to it. And Phil really enjoyed it. Saw it as a farce he had written and pulled off brilliantly. I saw then how I had never really known him. Only knew a charming actor. So, apart from thinking what a fool I'd been, it faded very quickly. I don't know why I didn't see through him. You and Val did, and tried to warn me.''

"He has great charm and good looks. He'll go through life skimming off all the cream he can, loving success, and probably getting in and out of scrapes with women, without suffering the least damage to his ego.''

"Val calls him the party man. It's apt, I think.''

"I'm sorry he hurt you, but romance is like a rosy veil, easily torn. Up against reality, it changes. Either to sex games, which I gather you resisted?''

"Yes.''

"Or to loving, which is a different category altogether.''

"I've learned that. Perhaps I should thank Phil for a salutary lesson. I thought I was unhappy about him until I saw Jean in your arms, and realised, or thought I realised, that she had taken my place. That was *my* all time low. I knew what real unhappiness was then. Made worse by the knowledge that I alone was to blame. Forgive me, Mark. I must have made you deeply unhappy, too."

"Yes. I'd claimed you when you were too young, perhaps. You'd been trapped in an unhappy home, had seen little of the world, and hungered for romance, which I was too familiar to provide."

He broke off and took her face between his hands. Then he kissed her and held her close, saying,

"I can't make pretty speeches, my love, but I'm glad you've come home!"

Lying there in the sun, the bitter-sweet scent of heather about them, the sound of bees seeking honey from the flowers, they lost track of the hours until they discovered that it was long past lunch-time and they were hungry. Happiness, thought Kate, looking up into Mark's dark face which bore an expression of tenderness which warmed her heart, is here and now. Hold it, cherish it. This moment she would always remember; the scent of heather, the hum of bees, the warmth of the sun from a cloudless sky and the face of the man who had loved her so constantly for so long.

Later, their hunger appeased, Kate, munching an apple, said reflectively, "You know, I've very poor judgment. Looking back to last Christmas, I had everything wrong then. I thought Philippe was all I'd dreamed of, Hugh quite impossible. Couldn't imagine why Evelyn had married him. Then, afterwards, I completely misread the situation between you and Jean, and have little understanding even of my own sister. Am I so blind?"

"That's a very harsh verdict," said Mark, smiling. "People are not so easily understood. You can peel them like an onion and still find unexpected qualities beneath each skin. I misread the situation between you and Phil latterly, and I've had more years of experience than you. Hugh was always worth ten of Phil, but I've known them both for a long time."

"I still think I'm lacking in discernment," she said ruefully.

"Well, I hope you feel you've got it right now."

She ruffled his hair and kissed him.

"Absolutely right. But it took me a long time along a very twisting path."

"Well, we'll be travelling together in future, and perhaps that will have a stabilising effect. We've wasted enough time, love. I'd like to break the news this evening and marry you just as soon as it can be arranged. After the frustrations of the past years, I refuse to contemplate a long engagement. I hope you feel the same."

"All I can keep saying today is yes."

He smiled and drew her to him.

"And a splendid word it is. I love you, Kate. I want you in my life, and I hope, and believe, I can make you happy. We know each other well enough to be confident about the future, I feel, or as confident as anyone can be in this chancy life."

He was thinking then of Jean and Darrel, she guessed, and held him tightly.

"I know we shall be happy together," she said, her cheek against his. "I know it."

*　　*　　*

They made a detour on the way back to take in a small town where Mark bought two bottles of champagne.

"We'll celebrate the last night of the holiday in style," he said. "Might even persuade Hugh to drink half a glass. Nuisance about his specs. Evelyn will have to drive them home. He didn't bring a spare pair with him. I find that amazing. Hugh always provides for every contingency."

"Dear Hugh. He's almost my favourite man. What an extraordinary holiday this has been! I feel I've been tossed about so much, I'm still not sure where I am."

"You're back with me, for good."

"You didn't want to come on this holiday, did you?"

"Communal holidays are not my scene. And to be under the same roof as the girl I loved and wanted, and who was as I believed still out of reach, spelt frustration and frayed nerves. But it's had a happy ending, and that's all that matters."

The sun was sinking as they neared the cottage, and the moors were bathed in a mellow glow. Kate, wrapped in a deep happiness as warm as the sun, wondered how she could ever have fallen for the tinsel charm of Philippe Touraine when the real treasure had been there for the taking.

"Well, let's face the music," said Mark when they arrived. "There will be no doubt about the family's approval. You've always been one of us, anyway."

"Val may be surprised, since our recent encounter wasn't exactly loving."

"She'll have to learn to duck the saucepans when she visits us."

A thought struck Kate as she got out of the car.

"Mark, you won't expect me to give up the business?"

"The decision will be yours."

"I can't leave Val now. Just as we're making our way. And I think I'd be wise to keep some measure of independence," she added, her eyes teasing him.

"Am I such a male chauvinist?"

"Underneath, yes. But a nice one. I think I can keep my feet. But don't think I shall hang on the Director's every word, like your secretary and housekeeper. You're abominably spoiled, according to Val."

"All I ask is that you don't let fly in the middle of cooking and spoil our dinner. Perhaps it would be a good idea to keep on Mrs. Sanders to housekeep. That business is a full time job for you, and I don't want you run ragged by trying to cope with home and job. That is, if you like her. She's a kindly soul and very loyal."

Kate looked at him, her head on one side, smiling.

"You've got it all worked out, my lord, I'm sure."

"Here, take these bottles," said Mark, holding the champagne out to her. "I've an urgent need to kiss you."

He took her in his arms, champagne bottles and all, and took his time in a long embrace which Evelyn and Valerie, emerging from the cottage, witnessed with interest.

Thus it was that the turbulent holiday ended with a happy, champagne supper and nobody denied Evelyn's claim that it had been a great success.

16
End of a Waiting Game

If the reception to the news of their engagement had been heart-warming from the Vermont family, it was quite otherwise with Pamela.

Kate, on a shopping expedition to London on her free day the following week, met her sister for lunch and broke the news to her when their coffee arrived.

"You must be crazy, Kate. You broke free once. Now you're back in the hands of that arrogant male. He'll take you over, body and soul. Haven't you learnt anything? You saw the real face of marriage in our own home."

"You're generalising from one disastrous example. To compare Mark with my father is ludicrous."

"You don't suppose Mother had an inkling of what life with him would be like when she married him, do you? It's all sweetness and light beforehand. Then snap, and you're trapped. I thought you were enjoying yourself with Philippe Touraine. Did he get bored with you and send you into Mark's waiting arms on the rebound?"

Pamela's tongue had lost none of its skill to hurt. Kate wondered if she knew how like her father she was. The father she had condemned so bitterly. The same cruelty, the same intolerance towards all who differed from their views.

She spoke calmly, however. "I'm not discussing it with you, since you're quite paranoid about Mark, for some reason. I know what I'm doing is right for me. I love Mark and he loves me. I'm only profoundly thankful that he waited for me while I went off on quite the wrong tack. It was too much to hope that you'd wish me happiness, I suppose."

"Quenched by domesticity. I can't be a hypocrite and go in for sentimental platitudes. But Mark Vermont always had you on a string. I was afraid this would happen when he manoeuvred you back into that family again. He has a certain male animal attraction, I grant you, and knows how to use it. He's the worst type of overbearing male. He'll make you give up the business, no doubt, to minister to his comforts."

"He has left the decision to me, and I shall carry on for the time being. When we start a family, it may be a different matter. That's for the future."

"Poor Kate. About to be submerged. I've seen it happen so often. Lively, independent girls transformed into drab, bored wives, unrecognisable after a year or two."

Kate, holding on to her temper with difficulty, said firmly, "Let's agree to differ, shall we, and drop the subject? The right sort of life for one person isn't necessarily right for another. You want success and power. I want to love and be loved. To belong. You always cite our home life as a terrible example. It was. But I always think of the Vermont family as a source of real and lasting support and happiness to all of them. If Mark and I can make anything as good, I shall be more than content with my life. That's my last word on it."

Pamela shrugged, her face unusually flushed, and sipped her coffee in silence for a few moments, then said, "When is this happy event to be? Soon, I expect. He'll want to clinch it while you're on the rebound from Philippe Touraine."

"The first day of October."

"Well, I'm afraid I shan't be at the wedding. I shall be away in John's constituency that weekend. We've some important meetings. By the way, John's made me a director of his family business."

"Does that mean you're leaving the political scene?"

"Oh no. I can manage both. The new appointment will mean that I can keep an eye on the business for John, relieve him of some of the responsibilities. His parliamentary duties leave him little time for the business, and things have been getting slack there. I shall have to take on a typist to help with the political side."

"It sounds as though your plate will be full. Congratulations on the appointment."

"Thanks. It won't be a bed of roses. The appointment of a woman director was not all that popular in some male quarters, but I think I've got the measure of my detractors. I can foresee some heads rolling."

The cold little smile on Pamela's face reminded Kate yet again of her father. Pamela would enjoy the in-fighting, the tactical struggles for power in the world of commerce as well as politics, in partnership with the man she had served with a loyalty mainly based on self-interest. She had the single-minded ruthlessness that led to success. And at the end of the day she would probably be wealthy and friendless. To Kate, it seemed a cold, harsh road her sister had chosen to follow, a road which she knew would carry them far apart. And the happier Kate's life was, the more estranged would Pamela be, for she needed Kate's failure to bolster her own philosophy, and would refuse to witness a happiness that challenged it.

When Pamela, pleading a business meeting, departed abruptly, Kate lingered on with a second cup of coffee, pondering on the particular spite which Pamela harboured for Mark. Had she once propositioned Mark and received a dusty answer, as Evelyn had once hinted? Had that male animal attraction she had mentioned once drawn her? Impossible to say. Mark had no liking for Pamela, had crossed swords with her on several occasions in the distant past, and he could be effectively abrasive. She sighed. She would never know, for Mark would never tell her, and Pamela was beyond her understanding these days, so cold and determined, so inaccessible.

When Mark came to the flat that evening, he studied her thoughtfully after he had kissed her.

"And how was Pamela?"

"As usual. Not what I would call an enjoyable lunch."

"I was afraid it might be a little dampening. Not seriously so, I hope."

"Nothing can dampen me just now. But the failure of all sympathy between members of a family does seem sad. She won't be at our wedding. I somehow have the feeling that we've parted for good now."

"I'm afraid I can't see that as your loss. Where's Val?"

"Gone to an art class she's just joined."

"Good. We can dispel any chilliness left over from that lunch, then."

And this they effectively did. When, later, they restored order so that they could greet Valerie with some semblance of sobriety, Mark said,

"Could you manage to get away from the shop next Saturday afternoon and come to our open day? I'm sure Jean will perform the ceremony competently, but I'd feel happier if she had someone there for support. I shall be tied up. Some boffins from France are interested in our fruit trials. I shall have to entertain them to lunch, and show them round. The opening ceremony at the library is scheduled for three o'clock. It's bound to be a bit of an ordeal for Jean. The first time she's been back since Darrel's death. I think she'd be glad to have you there with her."

"Of course. Val can hold the fort here, I'm sure."

"Thanks. Stay on and have a meal with me after I've seen off our visitors. I'll get Mrs. Sanders to leave something cold for us. I want to discuss a plan I've been working out for our house. Here's Val. Tell you about it on Saturday."

* * *

The Fenton Grange Horticultural Station was thronged with visitors on that sunny afternoon in September. Jean and Kate walked round the grounds before the opening ceremony, but if Mark had thought Jean needed support, she gave no sign of nervousness or distress, acting as guide to Kate with composure as she pointed out projects, many of which had been instigated by Darrel.

"There's too much here to show you half of it in the time

we've got, but I would like you to see the alpine garden, which was Darrel's special interest, and the research laboratories. You'll get to know it all yourself soon and be as interested in it as I was, I expect.''

"It's a large undertaking. A lot of responsibility for the Director.''

"Yes. Mark inherited a good team from Darrel, though, and he's a skilled horticulturist and a very competent administrator. Darrel thought highly of him. But it's a taxing job, holding it all together, and that's why I'm specially glad that Mark will have you to support him, someone to come home to and share things with. A private life. The Station could eat him up otherwise.''

The alpine garden was a vast rocky slope, broken up by streams and miniature waterfalls. From the highest point, Kate could see the tall figure of Mark among a group of men inspecting the fruit area. Away to her left, large glass-houses winked in the sun. The main building, once a country house, looked far too handsome and gracious to house a research laboratory, to which Jean now led her.

Arriving at the new library in good time, Jean took Kate round the shelves, pointing out some of the old botanical books with their beautiful illustrations, now of great value. As the time for the opening drew near, she said,

"Darrel would be very pleased with it. So spacious and light after the dingy little room that housed the library in his time. Thank you for coming, Kate. It's helped a lot. I feel today that I can say goodbye to it, hand it over, accept that I've vacated the premises. The new owners will do well by it, I know.''

And Jean's composure was unwavering as the small gathering assembled: members of the staff, a few visitors, and Mark, who made a short speech introducing Jean and paying tribute to Darrel. Watching Jean, trim and elegant in a pale blue suit, as she drew aside the cloth which covered the plaque inscribed to Dr. Darrel Brynton and declared the library open with a few appreciative words, Kate silently applauded her courage.

Then it was all over and Jean slipped away. She had to

collect Diana, she said, and Mark and Kate walked with her to the car park and waved her off.

"I'll be with you as soon as I can. We close at six. See you at the house if not before," said Mark, and gave her arm a squeeze as he strode off.

He had barely left her when she felt her shoulders caught from behind and turned to see Philippe's smiling face.

"Don't look so surprised," he said, and kissed her cheek.

"What on earth brings you here, Phil?"

"You, of course. Who else?" He waved a friendly salute to Mark, who had turned at the corner of the drive to look back. If he saw, he took no notice and disappeared.

"I don't remember telling you about this open day. Nor do I see why it should interest you."

"Still cross with me? Not really. A little bird told me that you would welcome a reconciliation if I'd make the first move. Now, Kate dear, I'm sorry I offended you. Let's make it up."

He had taken her arm and his dark eyes regarded her fondly.

"What little bird?" asked Kate coolly.

"We'll go into that later. I was told you needed me to come to the rescue. Here I am. Couldn't desert my Kate when she's in a tight corner, any more than she deserted me. One good turn deserves another, and all that. Anyway, I hate being bad friends."

"I don't understand what you are talking about."

"So I'm to be punished a little longer, am I? Not worthy of you. I'm parched. Could you lead me to some tea? That looks like a refreshment building over there. Then you can show me round this place. Quite a set-up, isn't it? Somehow, I'd expected something smaller."

There was nothing for it but to agree. Short of having a row in public, which she suspected he would quite enjoy, she could think of no way of dismissing him.

He put his arm round her shoulders as they walked past the main building towards the refreshment area.

"Please don't behave as though you owned me, Phil."

A Slender Thread

"Come, Kate, don't be so off-putting. I'm here to do you a good turn, at some inconvenience, I may add."

"I honestly don't know what you're talking about. You can explain over a pot of tea."

But in the tea-room, Philippe was recognised. Heads were turned. Smiles directed at him. Not conducive to a serious conversation, thought Kate, her exasperation increased by his apparently fond concentration on her to the exclusion of all the admiring glances thrown at him. Her embarrassment was furthered by the sight of Mark and a little group of men sharing a pot of tea in the far corner of the room.

"My cousin doesn't seem anxious to acknowledge me," said Philippe.

"He's entertaining some visitors from France in his capacity as Director here. Do you expect him to come up and bow to our tele-star?"

"Naughty. Claws. I shall start feeling aggrieved soon. I come out of my way to rescue you, and get a very chilly reception. Oh, certainly," he added with a charming smile as he signed the fly-leaf of a guide to the grounds proffered diffidently by a young woman, who retired, delighted, to show it to the other occupants of her table.

"This is ridiculous," said Kate. "Have you finished?"

"No. I want another cup."

"Then I'll leave you to bask in the admiring glances of your fans. I'll wait outside and you can explain to me there the reason for this charade."

He followed her in a few minutes, and she led him to the comparative seclusion of the woodland garden.

"Now, Phil. What little bird? What rescue?"

For the first time, he looked puzzled.

"I was told you'd been bullied into getting engaged to Mark once again. That you had weakly agreed because you were on the rebound from me, and now you were anxious to get disentangled, and would welcome the chance to join up with me again."

"Absolutely false. All of it. I'm going to marry Mark, I love him and I'm happier now than I've ever been in my life before. No need to tell me who the little bird was. Pamela."

End of a Waiting Game

"Yes. You mean there's nothing in what she said?"

He obviously found it difficult to believe that Kate could prefer any other man to him. Pamela had played cleverly on his vanity.

"Not a shred of truth. I'm sorry, Phil. You've been led up the garden path."

"But why?"

"To make trouble between Mark and me, perhaps. Pamela disapproves of Mark and my marriage."

"Spiteful. And I don't take kindly to being used."

"Nor did I," said Kate gently.

He looked at her quizzically, then he laughed.

"I asked for that. Dear Kate. Of course, she may have thought genuinely that I could have won you away. After all, I did before."

He looked at her hopefully, and Kate smiled as she shook her head.

"Not a hope, Phil."

"Oh well. A pity. I always had a weak spot for you. Not that I've anything against Mark. But . . . "

"You would be a better prize," suggested Kate, her eyes dancing.

He shook his head and gave a dramatic sigh.

"It was nice while it lasted. You should look out for that sister of yours. And I shall let her know that she's not my favourite character, either. Now I must go. Botanical matters don't interest me. I'm glad you're happy, Kate. I think you're well suited, you and Mark, after all."

Not sure whether this was a back-handed compliment or not, Kate walked with him to the car park and saw him shoot off in his red sports car. It was difficult to feel angry with him for long. But she felt very angry with Pamela as she walked slowly back wondering what Mark would have made of that encounter. Surely he wouldn't believe that there was anything between her and Philippe now. But she waited for him outside the Tudor-style house called Little Fenton on the perimeter of the Station grounds, which was so soon to be her home, feeling disturbed and a little uneasy at the turn of events.

A Slender Thread

The sun was warm on her face as she sat on the seat by the front door and watched the last of the visitors straggle towards the exit. There was no sign of Mark. As she sat there, the thought of Philippe's intrusion that afternoon buzzed round her like an irritating wasp. She had told Mark that all was over between her and Philippe, and yet he had turned up here and behaved as though they were still deeply involved with each other. How much had Mark seen? Little, perhaps, with his guests to look after. But she had broken off their engagement once, and he might not feel all that secure. He was not the man to relish having a rival hovering in the background of his marriage. Then she chided herself for making a mountain out of a mole hill. The truth was that the happiness of the past weeks so far surpassed anything she had known before that she had become nervous of losing something so precious.

Then she saw him coming from the direction of the car park. He was stopped by the short, sturdy figure of his assistant, and stood talking to him for a few minutes. Then, as he neared the house, a youth, one of the trainees she thought, stopped him. And at that moment, eerily, she felt as though she was looking at a stranger. A tall, strongly built man with black hair, formally dressed that day in a light grey suit, in charge of a world in which she had no part. Then he laughed and patted the fair-haired boy on the shoulder before turning away. In three weeks' time, this man coming towards her would be her husband.

"Sorry I'm a bit late," he said as he came up. "Our visitors seemed reluctant to go. You look as though you've seen a ghost. Anything wrong?"

"No, nothing at all."

He opened the door and followed her into the sitting-room.

"Quite a day. I could do with a drink. Sherry?"

"Please. It all went off splendidly, I thought. Jean never faltered. Played her part beautifully."

"Yes."

He lounged back in the armchair opposite her, his eyes studying her as he sipped his sherry. Lowering her gaze, she could not think why she was unable to behave naturally with him, why this strange gap had opened.

"That's a very pretty dress," he observed when the silence was becoming marked. "Willowy green suits you."

She smiled her thanks.

"What is it, Kate?"

"Oh, it's absurd," she said, suddenly impatient with herself. "Just that you seem to have become remote to me today. Like a stranger. I can't equate you with my husband to be."

His lips twitched as he put down his glass and held out his hands.

"Well, you'd better come and get acquainted again. It will be all right on the night, you know."

Sitting on his lap, his arms round her, confidence returned.

"Did you see Philippe?" she asked.

"He's not the sort of person one can very well miss," said Mark drily. "Why did he come and how did he know it was an open day here?"

"Pamela told him. I'd mentioned to her that Jean was opening the library. She also told him that I needed a reconciliation with him to extricate me from a marriage I was being dragged into on the rebound."

Mark's lips tightened, then he said, "I thought that lunch with Pamela might draw her fire. She never gives up, does she?"

"Why does she dislike you so much, Mark? I know she has a low opinion of men in general, but with you she is especially vindictive."

"We had an unusually frank exchange some years ago, and she's never forgotten, or forgiven. She's driven by demons, your sister. We should be sorry for her. How did Phil take it when you enlightened him?"

"A little cross with Pamela. But it's all water off a duck's back with Phil. I can't be angry with him any more. Just can't take him seriously. Philippe is . . . Philippe. The females in the tea-room enjoyed him."

"So I noticed. Do I seem less of a stranger now?" he asked, his fingers caressing the nape of her neck.

A Slender Thread

"Quite familiar again and very, very dear."

"You weren't afraid that I'd see anything menacing in Phil's act, were you?"

"A little uneasy. Our happiness is so wonderful, I sometimes fear for it."

"Foolish on all counts. I know you too well ever to doubt your integrity, and I'd have to be a blind idiot to doubt your love now."

After some little time devoted to underlining this, they came down to practical matters over their meal.

"We need more space for our laboratories, Kate, and have in mind using this house for the administrative block to free space in the main building. I don't feel I want this house to be our home. For me, it will always be Darrel and Jean's home. It's too big and too encircled by the Station. I'd like a more private home, and a house has come on the market just on the other side of the far boundary. Remote enough for us to feel private, and near enough for me to keep my hands on the reins here. I'd like to show it to you this evening. What do you feel about it?"

"As you do. I feel it would be difficult not to get engulfed in the Station here."

"Yes. We've a meeting to discuss it tomorrow. We'd have to start our married life here, while we're organising things, but if you like the house in question, we can probably get possession and do what wants doing to it before the spring."

They walked through the extensive grounds of the Station in the cool of the evening. An arboretum and a small stream marked the boundary, and Kate exclaimed with pleasure when she saw the house across the stream. With its mellow red brick enriched by the afterglow of the sunset, its leaded light windows winking, it presented an inviting face after the starkness of Little Fenton. They crossed the wooden bridge spanning the stream and came to the house through an overgrown garden surrounded by a tall beech hedge. Mark had the key, for the house was empty, the owner having died, and it was being sold by executors.

"I like it," said Kate when they had finished their

inspection. "It has a warm, friendly feeling."

"Good. I hoped you would. The garden's something of a jungle," said Mark as they looked down on it from an upstairs window. "The owner was a keen naturalist and left the garden wild to encourage birds and meadow flowers."

"I knew it had a kind owner. Felt it the moment I stepped into it."

Mark smiled and drew her to him.

"A romantic to the last. I'll never live up to it, you know."

"I'm not worried. Bridge Cottage will be a happy home, I know."

* * *

During the busy weeks which followed, it seemed to Kate that time telescoped and she found herself collecting her dress from the aunts two days before her wedding in a breathless state of bewilderment.

"It's all happened so quickly," she said, as she sat in the garden drinking coffee. "This is the first time I've drawn breath since our return from Yorkshire."

"Hardly a hasty marriage, though. A four year engagement, wasn't it? Can't blame Mark for wasting no more time," said Aunt Lucy breezily. "We'd begun to think we shouldn't live long enough to see you married."

Aunt Grace, hastening to smooth over her sister's tactless tongue, said, "It's lovely to have a wedding in the family, but you were quite right not to rush into it, dear. After that sad time you had with your home troubles and your mother's illness, you needed time to adjust. Mark realised that you weren't ready for marriage then."

So that was how they saw it, thought Kate. They had always behaved as though the engagement still stood. Perhaps it was inconceivable to them that anybody could not want to marry Mark, for he was a great favourite with the old ladies. But all she said demurely was,

"It was fortunate for me that Mark was so understanding."

A Slender Thread

Then she was carried off to try on her dress before packing it up. The aunts had eagerly undertaken the making of her wedding dress, short though the time was at their disposal, and had produced a lovely creation which again had the strange effect of making Kate feel that she was looking at a stranger in the mirror when she tried it on for the last time. Of simple design, with a tight bodice, long tight sleeves, and a full skirt of white taffeta embroidered round the hem, it fitted perfectly. She could imagine how Pamela would react to this picture in the mirror: the sacrificial lamb. Turning, thanking the aunts warmly for their achievement, she found herself wishing for the formalities to be over, to be alone with Mark, whom she had scarcely seen during the past weeks, starting their life together. Their wish for a quiet wedding had somehow not materialised, and many guests were now expected at Dilford church. Mark had acquiesced with humorous resignation. His relations were coming over from France, and colleagues from the Station expected to be present. It was all beginning to seem unreal, like a play.

A kindly autumn sun shone on their wedding day, and Kate carried away with her only fleeting impressions of the occasion while she herself still felt in something of a dream. She remembered the first golden leaves of autumn in the path from the church door when they came out. The sight of Philippe happily signing autographs by the lych-gate. The reassuring feeling of Mark's firm hand in hers as they drove to the reception at the Royal Swan. The sight of Valerie, picking up the long forget-me-not blue skirt of her bridesmaid's dress and running after the car when they drove away, her fair hair shining in the sun, laughing and calling good wishes, for she had somehow got trapped in the crowd as they left.

They flew to Berne from Gatwick and arrived at their destination in the Swiss Alps early that evening. Their room was high up in the hotel, and stepping out on to the balcony when they arrived, Kate was met with the sight of the snowy slopes of the Jungfrau dominating the landscape. In the light of the sinking sun, the slopes turned slowly pink as she watched.

End of a Waiting Game

"A fairy-tale scene. Now I know it's all a dream," she said as Mark came up behind her.

"Is that how it feels?"

"Yes. It has, all day."

"Then reality, Mrs. Vermont, is about to break in," he said, drawing her back into the privacy of their room.

* * *

During those two weeks in Switzerland, Mark was able to show her all the beauties of that country in perfect, calm autumn weather. He knew it well from a plant-hunting expedition he had once undertaken, and together they walked through alpine meadows, took the mountain railways to the high alps, explored the unspoilt villages round the lake, and each evening sampled one or other of the many inviting restaurants in Interlaken for a dinner which the mountain air and their own exertions enabled them to enjoy to the full.

On their last evening, Kate walked out on to the balcony to watch the Jungfrau transform itself in the light of the sinking sun, a sight she could never tire of, and leaning on the balustrade, reflected on the amazing changes which had taken place in her life within the space of less than a year. Last November Valerie had written her a letter inviting her for Christmas with the Vermonts after her long absence from them. Since then, she had gone into a completely new and unexpected business venture, had fallen in love with Philippe Touraine and out again, had gained a new friend in Jean Brynton, and had discovered real love with the man who was now her husband. A love that was deepening all the time, and had revealed to her a life of the senses scarcely glimpsed before, for Mark was a tender and ardent lover and had evoked responses from her that delighted him and amazed her.

He joined her now, and put his arm round her waist.

"Pity it's our last night. We must come back in June when the flowers are at their best in the meadows. Happy?"

"So happy. Words can't say. I was just thinking what an

A Slender Thread

incredible year this has been for me. So much has happened to me. I don't feel that I'm the same person as I was when Val invited me back to your home last Christmas. Tell me, Mark. Did you ever think our break was final?''

"What makes you ask that?"

"Oh, something the aunts said to me. Their whole attitude, now I come to think of it."

"It's a difficult question to answer, but no, I don't think I ever gave up hope that you would come back to me. I felt that the tie was so strong, that it must in the end prevail. At times, I admit, it seemed a very slender thread. You were away a long time. Val gave me news of you now and again, but I didn't know quite what to expect when you came at Christmas. But I found that first sight of you immensely reassuring."

"Did you? I can't think why."

"You looked so guilty when you first saw me, like a naughty child who has been playing truant. And the old easy friendship was there as though nothing had interrupted it. Did you never give me a thought during that time in London?"

"Many thoughts. A ghost at my elbow most of the time. And I felt strangely lost during those two years. In a sort of limbo. I needed that break, though, Mark. To take stock of myself."

"I realised that, after I'd got over the first shock and distress. I feared Pamela's influence, though, and was mightily relieved when I saw you, I can tell you. Then, heartless girl, you stretched that thread to breaking point again by your involvement with Philippe. But perhaps that was an old ghost that had to be laid."

"You've been very patient. I'll try to make up for it."

"I can play a waiting game when the stakes are so high. And you've more than made up for it already."

And looking back, Kate smiled to herself as she realised how cleverly he had in fact played that waiting game. The long interval when he had left her free, the enticing offer of the business partnership with Valerie which had tied her into his family so securely, and the unobtrusive way in which he had kept in being that slender thread. And she wondered how she could ever have doubted that they belonged to each other.

The pink glow had faded from the mountain now and the snowy summit lay pale and gleaming against the darkening sky. Below them the lights of Interlaken sprung up, and scattered lights among the lower wooded slopes of the mountains appeared, too, like distant stars. A horse-drawn carriage clopped past the hotel. Nobody, thought Kate, could have found a more romantic setting for their honeymoon. But romance was a word Mark did not encourage, and she had to admit that reality was far more satisfying. This time tomorrow they would be back in Sussex, facing the challenge of their future together at Bridge Cottage with confidence and love.

Something of her thoughts seemed to have reached Mark, for he kissed her cheek and said, "This is an idyllic place and we must come back as often as we can, but home has an inviting ring about it now. We'll have champagne with our dinner tonight and drink to the future, which looks very, very good to me."

And with this, Kate whole-heartedly agreed.